MW01592657

THE DEAD OF WINTER

The Best Chilling Tales
of William P. Robertson

INFINITY
PUBLISHING

Copyright © 2010 by William P. Robertson

ISBN 978-0-7414-6313-5

Printed in the United States of America

This is a work of fiction. Names, characters, places, and incidents either are the product of the author's imagination or are used fictitiously. Any resemblance to actual events or locales or persons, living or dead, is entirely coincidental.

Published November 2012

INFINITY PUBLISHING

Toll-free (877) BUY BOOK
Local Phone (610) 941-9999
Fax (610) 941-9959
Info@buybooksontheweb.com
www.buybooksontheweb.com

THE DEAD OF WINTER

In the dead of winter,
skies are black as a shroud.
The hillsides are bald,
glaring skulls
& the earth's jaw is rigid
with death's cold silence.
Wolves voice their loneliness
in amphitheatres of stone.
I'm cold, cold, cold, cold,
frozen inches
from the Bunsen burner of love;
frozen by the dead of winter;
frozen by those who shriek
from the dark blizzards
raging in my memory.

CONTENTS

ACKNOWLEDGMENTS

The stories and poems listed below were first published in the following books and periodicals: "The Dead of Winter," William P. Robertson's poetry collection, *Burial Grounds* (Triton Press, 1977); "Brittle Shadows," *Champagne Shivers* webzine; "Wide Spot in the Road," *Dominus*, Galati, Romania; "The Spirit of Catherine," *Stride*, Cheshire, England; "The Weight," *The Glasgow Magazine*, Glasgow, Scotland; "The Eighth Wonder of the World," *The Bradford Era*, Bradford, PA; "The Brown-Streaked Sidewalk," *A Time for Seasons and Holidays: A Creative with Words Celebration*, Carmel, CA; "The Goldenrod," *Prelude to Fantasy*, Minneapolis, MN; "Fetters and Chains," *The Black Abyss*, Philadelphia, PA; "The Price of a Pint," *Dark Starr*, Oceanside, CA; "The Crimson Tinge," *New Blood*, Ontario, CA; " "The Spirit of Catherine" also appeared in *The Pennsylvania Reader*, Wellsboro, PA. "Wide Spot in the Road" was published in *Vega Magazine*, Bloomfield, NJ, and in G.W. Thomas' *Flashshot* webzine.

Special thanks to David Cox for designing the front and back covers. The photo on page 43 was provided by Lanny Larson. The Death Machine and Ralph and Nettie Crossmire sketches are courtesy of the McKean County Historical Society. The Kinzua Viaduct pics were contributed by Dick Robertson. Wade Robertson snapped the author's photo that first appeared on the cover of *Waters Boil Bloody*, a poetry chapbook by William P. Robertson (Robyl Press, 1990). All other photos were taken by William P. Robertson.

THE SPIRIT OF CATHERINE

Excitement had me by the throat as I skidded along the mossy rocks bordering the headwaters of Five Mile Brook. Although I had left my car well before noon, I was now just nearing my destination. I had been so immersed in fishing for scrappy native brook trout that my exploration had taken far longer than I had anticipated. When I disassembled my fly rod and hightailed it upstream, the evening shadows had already begun creeping out from beneath the hemlocks.

The scabby cherry trees seemed blacker than I had ever before seen them. The wind also began acting like the plaything of a perverse magician. Although I was an experienced woodsman, I had difficulty pinpointing from which direction it came. Its howling seemed almost cyclonic in nature and was rising fast. In the fading light only my stubbornness pushed me onward. Finally, without warning, I stumbled through an orange screen of beech leaves and skidded to a halt on the shore of the blighted swamp I had been seeking.

Having no brothers or sisters to accompany me, I had hiked alone in the woods since I was twelve. Yet, even I couldn't help but shrink from the vile sea of muck and stagnant water that stretched before me in the twilight. Great bleached tree trunks reached finger-like from the fringes of this mire, while ghostly beaver huts glowed in the mist now forming over the deeper pools. The distant chant of the whippoorwill made my face grow cold beneath my beard. If only I had asked a friend to come along. If only I had a friend to ask!

So this is where Catherine perished. No wonder the old Swedes wouldn't venture out here at night. According to legend, the girl had wandered off to pick Christmas ground pine and got caught in a driving blizzard. It wasn't until the following spring that her corpse was discovered by trappers near this very spot. Neighboring farmers swear that her cries for help can be heard echoing from these dark swamps even today. My grandmother said she was a winsome lass, wild as a colt and always out walking alone.

How strong the wind has grown. Yet, the mist, if anything, is swirling thicker. I must leave this blighted place before my imagination gets the better of me. I must turn and take one. . .step. . .at. . .a. . .time. Just one step. Oh, God! I'm sinking. . .sinking!

Catherine? Is that you? My, your skin is so cold and smooth. You are a winsome lass. Now, we shall never again have to walk through this swamp alone. . .

WIDE SPOT IN THE ROAD

Gus Carlson reined his team of horses to a halt. Staring ahead down the desolate one-lane forest track, he could feel his scalp tingle as he contemplated the hemlocks that hemmed him in like the walls of a grave. Even on the brightest summer day it was an eerie road to travel, for little sunlight ever filtered into the narrow tunnel of trees. Today, Gus felt especially uneasy as he watched the thunderheads gather in the dark sky above and listened to the howl of the rising wind.

The horses seemed to share the farmer's uneasiness. Pulling a loaded buckboard up a five-mile grade should have tamed even the most spirited of animals. Yet, Gus suspected that the heavy lather on the black mare's flanks wasn't entirely due to physical exertion. The beast's nostrils were just too unnaturally flared as it stared off wild-eyed into the gloomy wood. Even the gentle gray rubbed uneasily against the traces and had to be prodded forward with an unusual amount of coaxing.

When the animals finally plunged ahead through the tunnel of trees, they broke into a full gallop. The buckboard jolted wildly down the slope with the farmer yanking the reins and crushing the brake for all he was worth. It wasn't until the frenzied beasts had bolted to the top of the next hillock that Gus managed to bring them under control.

Despite the biting October wind, Gus discovered that he was soaked with sweat. Perspiration poured from under his hat band and dribbled onto his spectacles. With annoyance, he peeled off his glasses, mopped a coarse handkerchief across his forehead, and then proceeded to survey the distance with near-sighted eyes. From his hilltop vantage point, he could barely distinguish the blurry road ahead as it threaded its way across an infinite series of lower hillocks that rose like waves from the hemlock sea. When Gus replaced his spectacles, he noticed an ant-like vehicle moving toward him up the road three knolls away.

As Gus watched the other vehicle disappear behind the second hill, he wondered how they could ever pass on a wood-lined road barely wide enough for his own buckboard. This thought had little time to register before Gus saw the object of his concern miraculously appear atop the second knoll. This time Gus had no trouble identifying the mysterious coach. It was somber, black, and unmistakably a hearse! It was drawn by six gigantic black draft horses that trotted along as if in a trance. How the brutes were able to pull that hearse three miles in three seconds was something Gus didn't care to ponder. Instead, he urged his own trembling team forward. Shortly after, to his surprise, he found a place to pull off the road and await the distant coach's arrival.

When the hearse disappeared behind the remaining hillock that separated them, Gus wondered why in ten years of traveling to market he had never before noticed this particular wide spot in the road. Nervously, he pulled at his beard and then at his watch chain. He produced an initialed timepiece that had been a gift from his eldest son, Herbert. The watch read one o'clock. It had to be later than that, Gus thought. He held the watch to his ear. It wasn't ticking. Had he forgotten to wind it that morning in his haste to get an early start? Gus twisted the winding knob and found it wouldn't move. While he replaced the broken timepiece in his pocket, a distant rumble of thunder made his horses fidget in the traces.

Gus waited for what seemed like an hour. When no vehicle appeared atop the distant knoll, the farmer muttered, "Where could that hearse have gone? There's no side road it could have taken. And this one's not wide enough to turn around on."

The winds rose to gale force and snatched Gus' hat from his head. As he whirled around to save it, he gasped in surprise. There, disappearing over the horizon *behind* him was the somber, black coach for which he'd been waiting.

Suddenly, the black mare reared up on its hind legs, and the gray emitted an almost human shriek. Gus barely had time to grip the reins before his team was off and running. It never slowed until the dirt track blended into the brick highway leading into Gus' own gate.

When the buckboard swirled up the drive, Gus' wife appeared at the front door of the homestead. Her face was wan and etched with sorrow.

Visibly shaken, the farmer got down from the wagon and walked absently toward his trembling wife.

"Gus," she said blankly. "I have something to tell you."

"Yes."

"Our son, Herbert."

"Yes?"

"H-h-he fell down the well. . .Drowned. . ."

"Around one o'clock?"

"Yes, why yes!" sobbed Gus' wife, burying her head on his shoulder. "How did you know? How *could* you know?"

THE WEIGHT

As Karl Anderson struggled with his burden, he felt his knees buckle beneath him. At this rate he would never reach the barn that stood three hundred yards across the orchard. Reeling against the nearest apple tree, he righted himself to more evenly distribute the weight on his back.

"Vhy?" he wondered aloud. "Vhy did I come out in the woods so close to dark?"

Karl was a strapping youth. At seventeen, he was already well over six-foot tall. His two hundred pounds of bulky muscle helped him perform even the most rigorous of normal farming chores. From pitching hay, to guiding a plow, to digging postholes, to shearing sheep, he was the first of his family to finish his work and the last to complain of fatigue. But then, the weight with which he now found himself saddled, could hardly be characterized as "normal."

If only he had not been so skeptical of the old legends. Those, like everything else Swedish, he believed should be cast aside now that his family lived in America. "Vhy dvell on customs from the old country?" he had asked his father countless times. "If you loved the old ways so much, vhy did you put an entire ocean between you and them?"

Karl had another more personal reason for spurning his heritage. He was tired of being the brunt of the

American boys' jokes. Often, his muscles had also come in handy when he ventured into town. At first, he had only used them when goaded into fighting by the taunt of "Dumb Swede!" That, however, was before he had thrashed every upstart farmhand within twenty miles and, in turn, had become the bully.

A faint tremor that most would have recognized as fear pulsed through the brawny lad as he again lurched toward the distant barn. He was soon forced to rest against every third tree he blundered upon in the growing gloom.

Sweat poured from the immigrant boy as he leaned panting against the rough bark of a hickory trunk. Closing his eyes, he was suddenly disturbed by a very real childhood memory. It was that of his grizzled Uncle Ole sitting hunched over in his favorite rocker croaking out tales of elfin lore. Face animated with firelight, the old man had delighted in frightening the children who gathered about the hearth to hear the stories he told every Midsummer Eve. The rest of the year he was seldom known to speak more than a few mumbled words. Too shriveled to work anymore, he spent most of his hours daydreaming or limping alone through the woods to gather herbs and mushrooms. These Ole used in medicines he concocted for all the old crones of the neighborhood.

By far, his uncle's favorite stories involved the trolls—those hirsute creatures reputed to haunt the dank woodlands surrounding the Anderson farm. Karl remembered how loudly he had laughed when Ole, in the midst of his narration, would twist up his bearded cheeks in impish imitation and leap at an unsuspecting child nestled at his feet. Then, the old man would describe in hideous detail how after sunset the Little People dropped from trees to steal a ride on a human's back. By the time Ole had explained the trolls' ultimate intent in doing so, all the children (but Karl) were crying in their mothers' aprons. These stories still would seem ludicrous if it had not been for the pig-like bristles scraping against the back of Karl's neck.

Karl reached the edge of the orchard just as the final glimmer of twilight was fading from the sky. Eyes blurring with fatigue, the Swede now viewed the barn as a mere shadow outlined against the horizon. With the building still a hundred yards away, he felt an overpowering urge to sink to the ground for a quick rest. Only the smell of bitterroot reminded him of the consequences.

With his endurance fading fast, Karl recognized the need for drastic action, and he became infuriated by the whole situation. After all, what had he to fear? Had his brawn ever failed him before in any wrestling bout? Certainly not! It had never mattered what type of death grip his opponent had used. Why should it now?

Karl reached one rope-like arm over his shoulder. Instead of throttling the unseen enemy as planned, he found his range of movement shackled by his huge expanding bicep. Howling in a blind animal frenzy, the immigrant whirled around and around like a bear swatting bees, clawing at the empty air. When he felt the weight grow tighter to him still, he wildly butted his back against the next gnarled tree he encountered in the dusk. Each time he rebounded into the air, a shock wave exploded in his brain.

Finally, everything went blank, and Karl slumped to his knees. The next thing he knew, he was instinctively stumbling in a dead run toward the barn. The brief contact with the ground had proven true his Uncle Ole's elfin lore. No blackout could compare with the empty nothingness of one's soul being slowly sucked away.

Karl was now totally consumed by fear. Nor had he ever before felt so alone. It was as if he were rushing headlong down a subterranean tunnel to hell. He could no longer feel his legs, but he knew they were working when the deeper shadows surrounding the barn loomed up to engulf him.

With the radar of a bat, Karl veered off at a right angle to the barn wall and followed it along until he distinguished the faint glow of lantern light leaking from the bottom of a side door. He lifted the latch and ducked his giant frame through the four-and-a-half foot opening that had been purposely built that height by his superstitious father. As he did so, he heard a thump behind him and whirled in time to see an impish figure leap up and flee into the gloom. All at once, the weight was gone from Karl's back. If only it had left his heart, as well. The imp had had his Uncle Ole's face.

MRS. BABCOCK'S ABC'S

It was late afternoon, and pudgy Perry Black sat alone in his second grade classroom. Even the casual observer would have seen he was scared. His red freckles stood out like chicken pox on his pale cheeks, and his hands twisted nervously in his lap. His teacher sure was taking her time returning from the principal's office. Knowing her sadistic tendencies, the boy figured that was all part of the punishment.

Perry stared at the clock above the door and saw that it was 3:22. He heard the last of the buses rumble out of the parking lot. Once they were gone, an eerie silence crept over the schoolyard. Inside, the building was even quieter. The prisoner squirmed listening to the distant rattle of the furnace pipes below him.

Now, my parents gotta pick me up, an' school ain't the only place I'll be in trouble, Perry worried. *Our farm's far out in the country, and Pa sure hates quittin' his chores to drive way into town. This time I'm gonna get a whippin' for sure.*

Perry's nose wrinkled in disgust while he pondered the source of his trouble — Mrs. Babcock. "What a nasty, old witch she is, anyway!" he grumbled under his breath. "If she ain't rippin' on me with that sharp tongue of hers, she's rappin' my fingers with a ruler. Even worse, she gives me so much homework I can't even play Peewee Baseball. I still don't see why Ma thinks 'ritmetic is more important than smackin' long home runs. There's no dang escape from Babcock's torture."

The boy also hated how dark his teacher kept the room. She never let in any sunshine. Last week she clawed him good when he tried to open the blinds and show her a rainbow he'd seen during recess. Now, the light was so dim, he could barely make out the print of the Dick and Jane book he was assigned to finish. He was behind a grade in reading as the hag was constantly reminding him.

There's no way to get back at old Babcock, either, the boy reflected. *She never sits down without checkin' her chair for tacks. An' crap! She actually **likes** the snakes an' toads I put in her desk. I'll bet she makes soup out of 'em. Yeah, and it only made her laugh the time I yanked out my loose tooth an' dribbled blood on her new pantsuit. I wiggled the tooth all day so I could pull it out when she bent over to get my math test after sixth period. Wow! Did she get excited seein' my blood. That was creepy!*

Today, in desperation for revenge, the boy had attempted to slip a rotten apple into Mrs. Babcock's lunch sack while she was in the hall gossiping with another teacher. The apple was so decayed that even the pigs wouldn't eat it. If his classmates hadn't burst out laughing, he'd have gotten away with it, too.

"All the sixth graders say Mrs. Babcock's a ghoul," mumbled Perry. "That's why she always comes to school before daylight and goes home after dark. But who can believe them? Sixth graders will say anything to scare a little kid. They also told me the principal sleeps in a coffin down in the basement."

Perry looked in his desk and took a quick inventory of his cache of weapons. There were two spit wad straws, a rubber band gun, and three bobby pin snappers. *These might keep away Dan the bully,* he thought, *but they sure won't protect me from that crone – Babcock.*

The boy continued to dawdle until the sound of hurried footsteps reverberated from the hall. By the time his teacher entered the room, Perry's nose was once again buried in his first grade reader. He had perfected his fake study techniques so he could even fool his mother. He felt he could carry this off long enough to be sent on his way home.

Mrs. Babcock glared balefully at her student. Seeing he was holding his book upside down, she screeched, "Dick and Jane would run much faster if they weren't standing on their heads!" To drive home her displeasure, she pinched Perry's fat cheek before returning to her desk.

Reddening, Perry flipped over his text and hid behind the cover. Even reading was better than looking at his teacher. Not only was she tall, gaunt, and ugly, but the lad hated how her bones showed through her transparent skin.

"Perry!"

The boy sat up with a start and found Mrs. Babcock scrutinizing him. It gave him the willies the way she kept staring at his fat arms. *Now, I know how the Thanksgiving turkey feels when Pa inspects its drumsticks before deciding whether to cut off its head,* Perry reasoned.

"What's the matter with you, boy?" snarled the teacher. "You haven't turned a page in five minutes. Have you forgotten how to read, or are you hatching another of those schemes of yours?"

"I ain't doin' n-n-nothin', ma'am," stammered Perry.

"That's obvious," croaked the cadaverous woman slyly as she yanked open her desk drawer. "I think it's time we reviewed our ABC's."

"A-A-ABC's?" bleated the scared lad.

"Yes, my devious, little fellow, *A* is for *apple*."

Perry swallowed hard as he watched Mrs. Babcock produce the piece of decayed fruit that he had tried to slip into her lunch bag. She took a bite out of the rottenest spot and then sucked a worm from the core like it was a strand of succulent spaghetti. After licking the brown slime from her lips, she said, "And *B*, of course, is for *boy*—a plump, tender boy for supper!"

Perry leaped up screaming and bolted for the door only to find Principal Thomas blocking his exit. The towering man smiled broadly to reveal a mouth full of sharp, yellow fangs.

From behind Perry echoed Mrs. Babcock's screeching laughter. "And then there's *C*," she cackled, rising menacingly from her desk. "I'll bet even you can guess what that stands for."

Perry glanced warily at his teacher and shook his head, "No." Then, he dodged back into the classroom just as the principal lunged to grab him.

"*Crimson* is the answer you're looking for," Mr. Thomas thundered, while he and Mrs. Babcock backed Perry into a corner. "Crimson is the color of blood—warm, tasty human blood."

RESCUE AT THE DEVIL'S DEN

"If someone would stop throwing gumdrops long enough to listen," barked tour guide Pitts, staring angrily at the smirking fat kid in the backseat of the bus, "I would like to tell you about the Valley of Death we are now entering."

"Yeah, throwin' stuff is rude, Stevie," said Gregory, elbowing the scrawny boy next to him in an effort to pass the blame. "Pay attention to the man. He knows everything about the Civil War. I'll bet he was at Fort Sumter when the first shot was fired."

Scoutmaster Morgan fixed Greg with a withering glare. Afterward, he growled, "You're not fooling anyone, Gregory Battles. I'll bet your granddad would be greatly disappointed in your behavior. Maybe I should call him when we get back to Wellsboro."

Greg glanced sheepishly at the furious scoutmaster and then muttered something behind his hand that made Stevie snicker. Only after Mr. Morgan stood and took a step toward them did the lads assume the proper decorum.

To avoid further conflict, Greg pretended to pay attention to the bearded Mr. Pitts when he gestured out the window and droned, "We are now on Crawford Avenue. To your left you will see a boulder-strewn hill called Little Round Top where some of the fiercest fighting took place here at Gettysburg. On Day Two of this epic battle, a determined group of Pennsylvania volunteers positioned on Little Round Top stopped an all-out Confederate assault meant to turn the Union's left flank. After repulsing the Rebels' charge, the troops of General Samuel Crawford counterattacked, drove the Confederates down the slope, and pushed them across the marshy valley bottom where you see Plum Run meandering along not far from this road. The fighting was grim and often involved bayonets and rifle butts when muskets misfired or couldn't be loaded fast enough. Some men's deaths were so violent and sudden that their ghosts were set loose to roam Gettysburg forever. Specters rose everywhere about this valley running red with soldiers' blood and are still seen today by those attuned to the supernatural."

As the scouts gawked out the windows to follow the guide's narration, Gregory pulled a thick rubber band from his pocket, stretched it to its full length, and snapped Stevie wickedly on the ear. The surprised boy's scream punctuated the historian's frightful tale of disembodied souls. His tears brought a shower of catcalls and taunts of "Do ghosts scare little Stevie?" Soon, chants of "P-o-o-r Stevie! P-o-o-r Stevie!" roared from every corner of the bus.

Red-faced, the tour guide howled for silence. It took the badgering of the scoutmaster and several adult chaperones before order was restored. Afterward, Mr. Pitts cleared his throat twice and yelped, "Off to the right, you will see the Rebel stronghold known as the Devil's Den. From this rock formation, Confederate snipers shot Union officers and artillery-men over a quarter of a mile away on the summit of Little Round Top."

"Yeah, right!" said Gregory while faking a cough. Then, he whispered to Stevie until a ripple of laughter replaced the glum boy's sullenness.

"What's so funny?" cried Mr. Morgan, leaping into the aisle. "I swear I'd like to throttle you, Steven Mack! What did Gregory say? Well?"

"T-t-that he could h-h-hit a Yank with his s-s-squirt gun from here, too. . ."

"Is that so, Gregory? Normally, we stop and allow our scouts to explore the snipers' positions at the Devil's Den, but your behavior has made that impossible. It's too bad your whole troop will have to miss seeing this amazing natural fort."

Again, all eyes fastened on Stevie Mack and Greg Battles. As the scouts screamed to vilify them, Mr. Morgan growled, "It looks like you boys don't want lunch, either. One more outburst and I'll see that's arranged."

In a gloomy silence, the bus wound around a sharp curve encircling the jumble of gray boulders splotched with lichen. This now forbidden landmark of the Devil's Den made every lad itch to climb the erosion-smooth rocks and worm through the crevasses. Every patch of brush and pile of boulders that could have hidden a single Rebel sharpshooter looked inviting. Stevie and Greg stared longingly out the rear window until the rock formation disappeared from view.

"Cripe, if we hadn't watched that keen battle this morning, I'd be ready to go home," whispered the fat boy to his pal.

"Yeah, the reenactors were great! Too bad we couldn'ta talked to them Yanks an' Rebs an' looked at their guns an' stuff. Everything they had was true to history accordin' to Mr. Pitts."

"I wish that dang Pitts was history," snickered Gregory. "Then, we wouldn't have to listen to all his Little Round Top and Valley of Death crap. I already know everything he told us, anyhow."

"Sure ya do. . ."

After rolling past a display of cannon, the bus entered a dense wood. Here, it circled past several more monuments and then braked to a stop before an impressive statue of a Union soldier. The soldier struck a confident pose with his left arm held akimbo. Gripping a long musket in his right hand, he stared off into the distance as if he'd just whipped the whole Confederate army by himself.

"What's that on the statue's hat?" asked Stevie.

"Looks like a hot dog in a bun to me," chuckled Greg. "I must be hungrier than I thought."

　　"No, Mr. Battles," corrected Scoutmaster Morgan. "If you bothered to read the inscription, you'd see it's a buck tail. It symbolizes the shooting ability of these men, who often survived by killing deer for food before the Civil War. The regiment wearing these tails on their kepi caps came from Northwestern Pennsylvania and is a proud part of our state's heritage. That's why we stopped here to show you this monument. I myself had a Bucktail relative who was wounded here at Gettysburg."

　　"Yeah, the Bucktails were excellent marksmen," agreed the tour guide. "They usually served as skirmishers for the Union army."

"What does that mean?" asked Stevie.

"It means they were scouts who went out looking for the Rebels and often encountered the enemy first. They were like today's elite Army Rangers."

"The Bucktails must have been real tough then, huh?"

"That's right, Mr. Mack," replied the scoutmaster. "Why, at Harrisonburg they ran smack dab into an entire Confederate brigade. Although outnumbered five-to-one, they killed General Turner Ashby and five hundred of his soldiers. It wasn't until half the Bucktails lay wounded on the ground that they were forced to retreat."

"Wow!"

"And at Antietam," continued Mr. Morgan, "they engaged the Rebels the evening before the main battle began. After being raked by wicked cannon fire, they chased the Southerners into the East Wood and had to lay there all night to hold the enemy at bay. The Bucktails distinguished themselves even further at Fredericksburg. While the rest of the Union army got whipped soundly by Robert E. Lee, the First Pennsylvania Rifles were the only Yankee troops to break through the Confederate lines stretched out on the high ground above the Rappahannock River."

"Who were the First Pennsylvania Rifles?" inquired a wide-eyed lad, tugging at the scoutmaster's elbow.

"I'm sorry. I didn't mean to confuse you. That's the other name the Bucktails went by, along with the Thirteenth Pennsylvania Reserves."

"But by the time they fought at Gettysburg, they had joined the Federal army," reminded Mr. Pitts. "They were then known as the 42nd Pennsylvania."

"Did the Bucktails fight the Rebs first in this battle, too?" asked Stevie.

"No, they were stationed near Washington when Lee's army began its invasion of the North, so they had a long, hot march to get here. After a week's trek, the Bucktails still had to hike all night to arrive in time to join the battle on Day Two. Can you imagine marching ten miles in wool uniforms, lugging heavy rifles, blankets, and haversacks, and then fighting a battle? And they didn't have much time to sleep, either!"

"Can't we eat now?" grumbled Gregory. "The only battle I want to win is with my growlin' stomach."

"A-w-w-w! First, let's hear why they built this monument for the Bucktails," pleaded Stevie, remembering the smack Battles had given him on his ear. "You can wait a little longer, can't ya, Greg?"

"I'm glad that you're interested," replied the guide with a wide smile. "The 42nd Pennsylvania definitely deserved to be recognized for its role here. The regiment held the extreme left flank of the Union line on Little Round Top and helped drive the Rebels from the summit back across the Valley of Death to the Devil's Den. It might have even chased the Rebs from there if darkness hadn't fallen. The regiment's colonel at one point was well in advance of the other charging Yanks, leading by his brave example—"

"Thank you, Mr. Pitts," interrupted the scoutmaster. "I hate to stop your fascinating tale, but I think we better have lunch before our own troops get too restless. This is also a good place for us to stretch our legs."

With an exuberant shout, the scouts leaped from their seats and pushed up the aisle, nearly trampling Mr. Morgan and the bearded historian in their stampede. The boys charged off the bus and romped about the Bucktail statue while the adults unloaded cardboard boxes stuffed with sandwiches, apples, bananas, cookies, and grapes. When the lads surged forward to be fed, a displeased chaperone observed wryly, "You'd think it was our boys who had marched all night to get to Gettysburg. They act like they haven't eaten since leaving Wellsboro yesterday morning."

"The way they're pushing, I'll bet they'd settle for slimy salt pork and weevily hardtack the Civil War soldiers ate," grunted Mr. Pitts.

"I'm just glad we're serving lemonade instead of Coca-Cola," replied Morgan, "or they'd want to reenact Pickett's Charge."

Just then, Gregory crowded up to the scoutmaster to get his lunch. "I'm sorry for throwin' stuff on the bus, sir," he mumbled. "I must have left my manners at home."

"Apology accepted, Mr. Battles. Now, move along. We have a schedule to keep."

Stevie Mack squirmed from the jostling mob next. His lunch box barely touched his hand when Gregory began herding him toward a small marker to the left of the Bucktail monument where no one else sat. The marker resembled a tombstone. It had a Bucktail cap and an epitaph carved on it. Greg scanned the inscription and then whispered to the boy he had corralled, "While the grownups are busy, why don't we sneak off to the Devil's Den an' eat?"

"But w-w-what if we get caught?" stammered Stevie Mack.

"We'll never be missed if just the two of us go. Come on. It's not that far."

"I-I-I don't know. . ."

"Hey, you wanna see where the snipers hid out, don't ya?"

"I guess. . ."

"Then, let's go!"

"Are you sure we won't get in trouble?"

"Come on, you sissy! Nobody'll notice."

"But I don't wanna go where all those d-d-dead guys were."

"Then, you better not sit here either," said Gregory, "because a Bucktail officer bit the dust on this very spot."

Stevie leaped from the marker he was resting against, and Battles led him along the fringe of the crowd that nearly engulfed the bus. Next, the two boys nonchalantly wandered down the road, using the mob to shield their progress from the swamped adults. They pretended to be interested in a neighboring monument erected from three huge boulders for the 5th New Hampshire Regiment. When no one yelled after them, they disappeared behind the monument and lit out for the Devil's Den.

The boys kept to the brush until they could no longer hear the impatient voices of the famished scouts. Returning to the road, they walked briskly along munching on sandwiches between triumphant snorts of laughter. While they finished their lunches, Greg stopped to inspect a display of field cannon and a monument featuring a Union artilleryman holding a ramrod.

"Come on!" urged Stevie nervously. "Let's get goin'! It looks like it's gonna rain."

"Keep your shirt on," grunted the fat boy. "My granddad used to be a battlefield guide here until he had heart trouble. He taught me all about Civil War cannons an' stuff. He knows way more than old Pitts. I wanna have a good look at these Parrots. Or are they three inch ordnance guns? Let me see. . ."

Stevie Mack continued to badger his friend while Greg inspected the field pieces. Ignoring Stevie's pleas, Greg pretended to load one. It wasn't until Battles pulled an imaginary lanyard and fired his cannon that he finally took to his heels. Despite his size, the boy could really run, and Stevie had a hard time keeping up. He chugged along behind the heavy lad until they bolted around a corner and spied the jumble of rocks they'd seen from the bus window.

"Wow! Them boulders are really high," gasped Stevie, staring at the rocks towering above him. "An' look at how many hidin' places there are. There are even walls made outta stones. No wonder they call this place the Devil's Den."

"A sniper hid behind those walls," explained Gregory. "He called them his 'home.' An' look! There's pit marks made by return fire. Ya know what kind of guns the Rebs used to shoot Yankees on Little Round Top, don't ya?"

"No."

"Target rifles that weighted over thirty pounds."

"Like your gut, ya mean?" razzed Stevie with a nervous laugh.

"An' they had long octagon barrels an' twenty power scopes. That's why those guns were so accurate."

"How do you know? You're just pullin' my leg, aren't ya?"

"No, I swear it's the truth. My granddad told me all about target rifles, too. I'm not really dumb. I just pretend to be. . .sometimes. Can you imagine how the kids would pick on me if I was fat *and* a smarty-pants?"

"We still have to visit the museum this afternoon. I'll bet we'll see a target rifle there. Maybe we outta get back now before we get left behind. An' look at that sky. It's gettin' b-b-blacker by the minute."

"No! No! Let's climb to the top of those rocks before we go an' get a real view of Little Round Top. We could pretend we're snipers and pop a few Yanks."

"I wouldn't wanna do that. After hearin' what Mr. Morgan said about the Bucktails, I'd rather be one of them than a dang Reb. Let's go back. Please!"

"Hey, I came here to climb these rocks, and that's what I'm gonna do!"

"But what if we fall?"

"We're not gonna fall. Are you a baby, or what?"

With a haughty shake of his head, Gregory started up a gentle incline that led to the top of the first set of boulders. When Stevie saw how easy the path was to climb, he clambered behind his friend and reached the summit without breaking a sweat.

"Wow! That sure was a long way them snipers had to shoot," croaked the smaller boy, staring at the rocky hill across the valley. "I think our guide said it was a quarter of a mile."

"That's why I'll bet the braver Rebs went out on the next point," said Battles, gesturing toward the rock ahead.

"But they'd have to jump across that c-c-crevice to get there. It has to be f-f-five feet wide!"

"Ahhh! Anyone can make it if he doesn't look down. The way you whine like a girl, I wonder why I hang out with you. I think I'll start callin' you 'Stevena.' "

"Who are you callin' a girl? I can run an' jump better than most guys in my gym class. Coach Green even says so."

"Well, go ahead. Prove it!" dared Battles. "Jump over to that other point. It's flat as a tabletop. Even Stevena can't get hurt landing there."

"Okay, I will!"

Stevie measured the jump across the wide crevice with his eyes. After brushing away some loose gravel that littered the ledge, he backed up to get a running start. With a determined cry, he shot forward and leaped with all his might toward the flat point ahead. He flew across the deep fissure and landed on his feet well beyond it. He put on the brakes and stumbled several feet farther before coming to a halt inches from the cliff at the end of the rock formation. Afterward, he spun around and stammered, "I-I-I did it, Greg. Now, it's your turn."

"Not before you leap back over here again," replied Battles with a weak grin.

"Back?"

"Yeah, it's not smart for both of us to get trapped out there."

"Trapped?"

"I was just teasin'," confessed Gregory. "I didn't think you'd really jump."

Looking toward his friend, Stevie saw that the rock he was on was much lower than the one he had jumped from. In order to return to safety, he had to leap over the crevice and up to a two-foot higher ledge. His mouth flew open at the discovery, and his legs turned to water. With a deep groan, he melted to his knees and cried, "How am I gonna get offa here? How? How?"

"Don't ask me," replied Gregory, helplessly kneading his hands. "Maybe I oughta get help."

"Hey, don't l-l-leave me!"

"But it's startin' to rain. You'll never get off those rocks once they get slippery."

"Slippery?"

"You heard me. I gotta go."

Before Mack could further persuade him, a rumble of thunder sent Battles scurrying for the path that led to safety down the back of the Devil's Den. He had no sooner disappeared from Stevie's view when a heavy downpour began to pound against the rocks. It was followed by flashes of lightning from across the Valley of Death. Remembering a page from the scout handbook, Stevie immediately flopped on his belly and flattened himself out of the rock.

The boy burst into tears as the cold rain pummeled him, and a gusting wind whipped his drenched clothes. Shivering uncontrollably, he blubbered, "I gotta get off this point. I just gotta!"

Stevie continued to sob until he saw a tall figure emerge on top of the ledge recently vacated by Battles.

The man was dressed in a stained, tattered uniform of Yankee blue. He had a youthful face and kind, hazel eyes. His dark hair and goatee made his fair skin look even more pallid. Despite his youth, the soldier carried himself with an air of authority that caused Stevie to notice the colonel's eagles sewn on the shoulders of his uniform.

"It looks like you got yourself into a pickle, laddie," shouted the young officer. "Don't worry. I'm here to help."

"You a Bucktail reenactor?" cried the boy, seeing the white tail sewn on the colonel's kepi cap.

"Yes, I'm a Bucktail. Fred Taylor to be exact."

"I'm S-S-Stevie Mack. Everybody's gonna call me 'Stupid' when they f-f-find me."

"Don't run yourself down, laddie. You jumped out there on a dare, didn't you?"

"Yes, sir. How do you know?"

"I did plenty of foolish things myself for the same reason. I couldn't seem to help it. I was impetuous by nature. Like the time I gave myself up to the Rebs at Harrisonburg to tend the wounds of Colonel Kane. I was just a captain then and took some real kidding from the Bucktails after I got exchanged."

"Wow! You take your reenacting seriously. I watched your battle this morning, and did it look real with the cannons blastin' an' the smoke rollin' an' the bayonets shining in the sun. All the hand-to-hand fightin' looked real, too. You must be really brave."

"And I'll bet you're a brave lad, too, Stevie. You're related to Samuel Mack, aren't you?"

"How do you know I had a great uncle Sammy?"

"I knew him back in '61, and you're his spittin' image when he was a might younger."

"And you say he was brave?" asked Stevie as the rain stopped and the sun burst through the clouds like a glowing ball of fire.

"Didn't you know he fought at Gettysburg? After we chased the Rebs into the woods over yonder, it was your uncle who went forward to scout out their position just before it got dark. After all the fighting he'd been through that day, he wanted to make sure the enemy didn't outflank the rest of us Bucktails and cut us to pieces."

"You say I look like him?"

"Yes, an uncanny likeness. Now, let's get you back to safety."

"A-a-are you sure you're up to it?" stuttered Stevie, noticing the deep crimson stain on the breast of the other's coat. "Did you hurt yourself in t-t-today's reenactment?"

"Just a scratch, laddie."

"Okay. I guess I'm r-r-ready if you are."

"Then, get up and walk to the far end of that point. It shouldn't be slippery now," said the colonel, pointing to the steam of evaporating moisture rising from the rocks in the sunshine.

Stevie wobbled to his feet and took one fearful step. When his canvas sneakers didn't slide, he took another and another until his confidence returned. With a weak grin, he walked as far as he dared toward the end of the point. After what seemed like an eternity, he turned to face the colonel, who continued to shout encouragement.

"All right, Private Mack. When I give the command, run as fast as your legs will carry you. Remember. Jump high. Go!"

Stevie tore across the top of the rock. He rushed through the rising steam until he was at the very brink of the crevice separating him from the beckoning officer. Then, he launched himself into the air and flew toward the other ledge. He hit the opposite rock with a terrific thud that knocked the air from his lungs. His toes churned in the loose gravel, and he clawed for a handhold on anything that would keep him from pitching backward into the yawning fissure he had cleared by only a couple of inches. He felt himself sliding backward into the abyss when a pale hand shot out and dragged him to safety.

For many minutes Stevie Mack lay shivering. Pain throbbed through his skinned knees and elbows, and his heart pounded from his close call. When he finally looked up to thank his rescuer, he found himself alone on the rocks.

Still trembling, the lad staggered to his feet and peered down the backside of the Devil's Den. Below him, he saw the tall colonel striding toward the path that led to the Bucktail Monument. Before Stevie could yell to him, the soldier vanished into the thick woods.

Blinking back tears, the boy tottered down the incline leading from the jumble of rocks. He hadn't gone far before he heard voices rushing toward him. The next minute he found himself being mobbed by Gregory Battles, Mr. Morgan, and a dozen scouts.

"So ya saved yourself, did ya?" shouted Greg, slapping his friend wildly on the shoulder. "Ya saved yourself! Saved yourself!"

"I'm so glad you're okay!" cried the scoutmaster with a relieved grin. "Why, you're soaking wet. That rain sure came down. Here! Throw this blanket around your shoulders before you catch a cold."

"D-d-did any of you see a Bucktail soldier?" asked Stevie through chattering teeth. "H-h-he was headed right toward you."

"We didn't see anyone," said Battles.

"But you musta passed him," insisted the lad. "I saw him come this way."

"Passed who?" asked Mr. Morgan, handing Stevie a thermos of lemonade.

"Colonel Taylor is who. He's the one who saved me."

"Colonel Fred Taylor?" gasped Gregory, his fat face turning suddenly white. "That can't be!"

"What do ya mean it c-c-can't?"

"We sat at *his* memorial before we sneaked off. Taylor was killed here in the woods on July 2, 1863. . ."

THE BROWN-STREAKED SIDEWALK

As the three boys squeezed through the crowd and out of the circus tent, their air of gaiety vanished. They had just spent two joy-filled hours giggling at clowns, oo-oo-ing at trapeze performers, and clapping (between big bites of cotton candy) at the elephant acts. Now, the time had come for the long trek home across town in the dark.

Buster, the eldest, assumed command once they left behind the smoky brilliance of the Big Top. He was a hulking youth of thirteen, and a sadistic grin gleamed briefly on his rough features as he glanced back at his younger brother, Lenny. The little squirt had his ball cap crammed down over his forehead, concealing all but his very round eyes. Dogging the heels of Buster's pal, Pete, he concentrated fully upon tracing the older boys' footsteps in the growing gloom.

Being a tag-along was about all that Lenny was good for. It seemed to Buster that he couldn't go anywhere without the little goof. And what made matters worse, their mother now expected him to drag Lenny along at night, too. Cripe, how were he and Pete going to meet girls if they had to wet-nurse the Squirt all the time? Well, maybe if everything went as planned on the way home. . .

To reach the distant lighted street, the boys had to cross a parking lot bordered by an abandoned baseball stadium. This ballpark once housed the Pony League team noted for developing such pitching stars as Elroy Face and Warren Spahn. But there hadn't been a night game there for years, and now its peeling green walls and ramshackle clubhouse created a pool of midnight that even quickened patrolling policemen on their rounds. Needless to say, the boys avoided these deeper shadows as long as possible while circling the outer perimeter of the stadium.

Finally, they arrived at a murky tunnel that ran between the left field wall and a boundary fence. Here, Buster winked at Pete before deliberately quickening the pace. The moment they were totally immersed in darkness, they were off and sprinting for the safety of the streetlights, two hundred yards away.

It took Lenny awhile to realize he was alone in the dark. He fumbled blindly along, groping for Pete's shirt sleeves and whimpering softly to himself. Ten steps into the blackness, he finally dared peek out from under the brim of his ball cap.

A squeal pierced the night like a hatchet blade. Pete and Buster nodded meaningfully to one another and then glanced up from where they stood panting against a lamppost. It wasn't long before they perceived a dim shape streaking around the corner of the stadium toward them.

Lenny emerged from the shadows hatless and out of breath. His face was pasty. His eyes glittered with fear. He gave no sign of recognition as he wheeled toward the older boys. If they hadn't grabbed him, he would have barreled into the path of an oncoming Studebaker.

"What ails you?" howled Buster as he struggled to restrain his brother. "Where's your hat?"

Lenny stared wildly at his captors and then nodded toward the eerie, dark tunnel.

"Hey, Squirt, you're not gonna leave it there, I hope. When we get home, you'll get a lickin' if you do!"

"I d-d-d-don't care!"

"Say what?" bullied Buster. "Why, I. . .I think you're chicken!"

The squirt flinched at the most dreaded word in a small fry's vocabulary, but he did not deny the accusation. Instead, he anchored himself to the lamppost in anticipation of his antagonists' next move.

"Don't tell us you're afraid of the dark," smirked Pete. "Are you scared the boogeyman will get you?"

"Yeah, if you think you're big enough to hang out with us, you'd better get your butt back in there and get that hat!"

Except to tighten his grip on the lamppost, Lenny still did not move. Only after contemplating the murder in Buster's eye, did he squeak, "Okay. . .but you gotta go with me."

The older boys glanced warily into the pit of blackness bordering the stadium before echoing, "Go with you?"

"S-s-sure. . ."

"You gotta be kiddin'," muttered Pete.

"Ah, heck!" growled Buster, staring red-faced at his watch. "It's gettin' late. Forget the cap. Let's just get outta here."

When Lenny, Pete, and Buster dashed from the stadium parking lot, it was already well past eleven o'clock. Now, instead of taking the long, safe way home, they were forced to cut through the town oil refinery to make up for lost time. Straying from the well-lighted boulevard, they stumbled along a set of greasy railroad tracks between oil tanks two stories high. As they moved farther into the complex, refinery towers loomed large, hissing steam and casting flickering flames across their path. With each new flare-up, Lenny dug his claws into the back of his brother's jacket and shut his eyes until they hurt. He was too scared to notice Pete's similar reaction.

Finally, even Buster could take it no longer. Catching a glimpse of the streetlights at the far end of the refinery yard, he shook his brother loose and broke into a gallop with Pete close behind. By the time the bawling Lenny had caught up with them, Buster was as self-composed as ever and standing on East Main Street. "What took you so long, Squirt?" he sneered.

Lenny dug his dirty knuckles into his eyes, precipitating a fresh flood of tears. "Why did you guys leave me back there?" he blubbered.

"Ah, shut up, you baby!" snarled Pete.

"Yeah," said Buster. "What are you gonna do when we get to the witch house if you're scared now?"

"W-w-witch house?"

"You know. The one at the end of the block. Gee, I thought all big boys heard of that place."

The house to which Buster referred had terrorized town kids for decades. It sat isolated on a bank overlooking East Main Street and was in a sorry state of disrepair. The porch was rotten, the shutters hung at crazy angles, and only the attic window was intact. It was there that "many a witch sighting" had been made, according to Pete.

"Yeah," added Buster, wishing to enlighten his brother. "Let me tell ya all about it."

And tell him about it, he did. For the next twenty minutes, as they scurried along the gloomy tree-lined street, the bully conjured up tales of evil-eyed hags and disappearing neighbor boys that left Lenny a quivering mess of twitching nerve ends. When at last they reached the opening in the trees occupied by the witch house, Buster was just finishing his ghastliest tale of all. With a wicked smile, he pointed up the hill and said, by way of conclusion, "And up there, in that very window, they could see the old witch hacking up Jimmy Jones' body with a butcher knife *this* long!"

Buster made an exaggerated gesture and then glanced in the direction he had just pointed. When his eyes focused on a green face leering at him from the attic, he heard Pete gurgle a warning before sprinting off down the street. The hairs on Buster's neck bristled, and he leaped straight in the air. The next instant, he was streaking in the same direction taken by his pal.

Halfway down the block Pete again came into sight, and Buster began to gain steadily on him. Just as he was about to overtake him, he felt a rush of wind and looked up to see the little squirt, Lenny, zoom past and disappear up the next hill.

Blinking with astonishment, Buster muttered, "What the. . .How the. . ."

It was then that he noticed the brown streak up the sidewalk.

THE CAR WRECK

It was Christmas Eve, and a blizzard whipped down the Tuna Valley, turning Route 219 into a Slip-'N'-Slide. Swirling snow enveloped the little village of Limestone, dimming all but the brightest stage lights beaming through a barroom window. Rock 'n' roll pulsed through the walls there, and a raucous crowd cheered and whistled between every song.

When the music finally ended at midnight, three inebriated, long-haired teens staggered from the smoky den and weaved across the parking lot to their snow-covered Ford Maverick. After brushing off the windshield with their coat sleeves, the drunks clinked beer bottles in celebration and squeezed into the front seat. Spraying other partygoers with slush as they fishtailed out onto the road, they howled with mischievous glee. Then, they blasted off for Bradford.

"Wow! Was the Nail packed, or what?" jabbered Eddie Miller, taking a swig of his brew.

"That's 'cuz the Orbit rocks hard, Pie Man!" blared a short, sloshed, muscular dude. "All the groovy people wanna see that band."

"Yeah, Gator, they played everything from Hendrix to Crazy Elephant. They're outta sight!"

"An' what a smokin' version they did of Spirit's 'I Got a Line on You,' " yelped Willie Lockwood, the driver of the Maverick. "When the guitarist ripped into his solo, I thought his amp was gonna blow!"

"Yeah-h-h!" wailed the other boys in unison, again clinking their beer bottles together. "Yeah-h-h!"

The pals' rousing cheer had barely faded away when the Maverick veered sharply toward the oncoming headlights in the northbound lane. Just before they rumbled across the medium, Willie finally remembered to grab the wheel.

"Hey, watch what you're doin'," squeaked Pie Miller, yanking another Schlitz from the six pack in his lap.

"You mean ya don't like my drivin'?" cackled Lockwood, punching the gas so the light rear end of his vehicle slid dangerously toward the guardrails.

"Naw, you're doin' fine!" howled Gator. "God protects all drunks an' fools."

"Then, we're doubly safe," chirped Pie, glaring at the driver.

"Ah, lighten up, will ya? I'm jess havin' a little fun."

The storm suddenly doubled in ferocity, and Willie completely lost sight of the road ahead. Instinctively, he pumped the brakes and slowed his Maverick to a crawl. Then, he madly tromped on the floor switch to cut his headlights to low beam. With the glare eliminated from the swirling snow, he spotted the ghostly gleam of taillights several yards in front of him.

Lockwood had just regained his bearings when out of the squall appeared a wispy figure hitchhiking along the drifted berm. After wiping the steam from the windshield, Willie bellowed, "Hey, ain't that Jeff Green?"

"Sure looks like 'im," affirmed Pie, "but I thought he was in Viet Nam."

"Better stop an' see," urged Gator. "It's a hell of a night for anyone ta be out there."

Lockwood decelerated the Ford and pulled alongside a tall, young man dressed in Marine dress blues. The soldier sported a buzz cut. He wore no gloves. He looked absolutely numb when Pie threw open the passenger door and invited him to squeeze into the backseat.

"Hey, good ta see ya, Jeffery," said Miller, reaching to shake hands with his old pal. "Man, are your fingers cold!"

"And look at how pale ya are!" exclaimed Gator. "Get in here before ya freeze your face off."

"Anything's better than dodging through rice patties with Charlie blazing away at you," droned the lance corporal. "It's a jungle out there all right, and it's filled with trip wires and buried explosives."

"So you have been to Nam," declared Pie. "It sounds like ya had a really rough time. How about a brew? That'll take your mind off the war."

"No. I'm still recovering from a stomach wound. That's why I got shipped Stateside."

"How'd ya get hit?" gasped Willie, gulping the Schlitz Eddie offered him.

"I was in a bunker when Charlie overran our camp. We were operating a few clicks from Da Nang in a clearing the flyboys napalmed just a few days before."

"If I get shipped to Nam, I hope I get stationed at Duc Lo," joked Gator, "'cause that's what I'd do the first time the Viet Cong attacked."

"That's not funny!" snapped Green. "If our sentries hadn't been trippin' on acid, I wouldn't have taken shrapnel from the grenades Charlie dropped on my squad. My sergeant wasn't so lucky. He had both his legs blown off."

"Yeah, I guess we're the lucky ones," confessed Lockwood. "All o' us got college deferments."

"I did, too," mumbled Jeff, "until my roommate at Clarion ratted me out to the dean."

"What'd ya do?" snickered Gator. "Have a group grope with the cheerleading squad? I remember you were quite the skin hound in high school."

"I hid a quart of Boone's Farm in my ceiling, is all. Damn Dudley, that wussy, thought we'd both get busted if I drank wine in the dorm. Next day, the campus fuzz showed up and went right to my stash. Only my roomie knew where I kept it besides me. Got expelled then and there. The draft board was more 'n' happy to give me a new vocation, so I beat 'em to it by enlisting in the Marines."

"What a bummer," wheezed Pie. "You sure had a lotta tough breaks."

"Hey, but at least you're safe now," reminded Gator. "And tomorrow's Christmas!"

"You're home with your old buddies, too," slurred Miller with a maudlin smile. "You're welcome to go to the Nail with us anytime to hustle chicks. Man, you had all the babes fightin' over ya in high school!"

Willie was about to make a lewd comment about the girls Jeff dated when he saw emergency lights and red flares glowing on the highway ahead. Instead, he muttered to his passengers, "Better hide them beers."

The driver exhibited surprising sobriety as he reduced speed. Alertly, he stared through the windshield until he spotted a demolished Chevy blocking the road. The car had obviously spun out of control, rolled over several times, and came to rest on its roof. Its wheels were now facing the sky and spun haplessly in circles.

Willie watched aghast as state cops and county mounties swarmed around the smashed vehicle like bees from a broken hive. Finally, his eyes widened in recognition, and he croaked, "Hey, Jeff, ain't that your old man's vehicle all smashed to hell? Jeff? Jeff?"

Lockwood glanced tentatively in the rearview mirror, and his hippie locks stood straight up on his head. After blinking in disbelief, he finally worked up the courage to turn and glance behind him. At that moment he heard Gator and Pie Man gibber in sheer terror. Then, he knew his eyes didn't betray him, for Jeffery Green *had* vanished from the backseat.

CAN YOU GIVE ME SANCTUARY?

Bobby Frederick's parents were at it again. He could hear them rumbling at each other through his locked bedroom door like two warring thunderheads. Lately, their squalling had become a nightly ritual. It seemed that the smallest thing would set them off. Planning next evening's dinner menu, rooting for different contestants on *The Price Is Right*, or bickering over the last beer in the fridge, inevitable ended in an all-out screaming match.

"Oh, well," the boy sighed. "Still one place to go. Still one place to go."

Bobby leaned over, flicked on his lamp, and then crawled out of bed. Crossing the room, he stopped in front of an antique bookcase that sagged beneath the weight of an incredible rock 'n' roll album collection. These records provided the boy with much more than a pleasant pastime. Over the years they had become his panacea and religion. Their power chords pumped up his confidence, and, on nights like this, they formed a shield against the horrible howl of his parents' altercations.

Of all the albums in Bobby's collection, it was those of the Doors that he held in special reverence. Unlike his friends, he had not bought the records to be cool. There was something about the group's eerie, organ-mad music that spoke of eternal sadness. What really hooked him, though, were Jim Morrison's tormented vocals. Every time he heard the singer's anguish, Bobby knew that there was someone else who understood why he locked himself in his bedroom every night.

Bobby was introduced to the first Doors' LP at a stoner party he attended. He had only gone to defy his father, not because he smoked weed. Even before he heard one note of the record, he was totally enthralled by the cover art—a photo of the musicians' blank, staring faces superimposed on a dark background that shrouded them in total mystery. By the time the radio staple, "Light My Fire," blasted from the speakers, Bobby had already heard five incredible songs dripping with sex and dark imagery. It was "The End," though, that voiced the same growing alienation that was eating at the very core of his being. The song wove in and out of his head for eleven minutes and thirty-five seconds as Morrison unraveled a stark tale of Oedipal lust and mayhem. Its psychological stream-of-consciousness mind trip was the most powerful experience of Frederick's young life.

After that, the release of each subsequent Doors' album became a major event to Bobby. He would haunt the local record shop for weeks until it finally arrived. Then, the record would remain on his turntable until he could growl out the lyrics to each song verbatim. It was after he had so digested the Doors' second disc, *Strange Days*, that the boy let his hair grow down to his shoulders. He also bought his first pair of leather pants. Morrison's vision of life's unreality had won him a new disciple in spades.

But it was the *Waiting for the Sun* LP that cemented Bobby's Doors fixation. Its message of overt revolution and sensuality transformed him forever and spurred a dark quest for freedom. "Hello, I Love You" ignited an obsession with two hippie chicks that he shadowed every evening after school, aching for wild, debauched nights of sex and discovery that Morrison himself so reveled in. Then, "Yes, the River Knows" fueled a drinking problem Bobby only concealed by withdrawing further from his family. When his father started in on him about his appearance or strange behavior, the boy would scream out the words of "Five to One" and bolt from the dinner table. Morrison's politically charged lyrics no longer allowed Bobby to tolerate the older generation's power trip. It was after one such act of open rebellion that Frederick began wearing a single strand of Indian beads around his neck in emulation of his shaman — Jim.

Tonight, Bobby's sadness went much deeper than usual. He turned off his lamp and plugged in the black light that hung over his bed. His wall-to-wall Doors posters sprang instantly to life. In their ghostly glow, he selected the *L.A. Woman* album from its protective sleeve. As he placed it on the turntable, he made sure not to smear greasy fingerprints on the grooved vinyl. To do so would have been like tearing a page from a holy text.

Bobby cranked up the volume until the walls shook. He still couldn't believe that Morrison was gone! None of the facts of his death made any sense. How could the Word Man have had a heart attack while relaxing in the bathtub? And how could anyone be sure he was even in the coffin they buried at Pere La Chaise Cemetery? After all, only his wife Pamela and the mysterious doctor who signed Jim's death certificate had actually seen the body.

Bobby lay back on his bed and let the music wash over him. Neither the raucous rock of "The Changeling" nor the happy groove of "Love Her Madly" alleviated his pain. When he chanted along to the guttural blues of "Been Down So Long," he thought the words had never seemed more appropriate. Gripped by the powerful vibe, the boy leaped to his feet, his clenched fists upraised. Then, he snatched a pool cue from the corner and wielded it like a microphone stand as "L.A. Woman" exploded into his consciousness. He continued to writhe trance-like in perfect imitation of the Lizard King until the hot, hypnotic beat faded from the room.

Bobby turned the album over, flopped back on his bed, and closed his eyes. There was an angry rapping on his bedroom door, but the threat was thwarted by the booming vocals of "L'America." The songs that followed allowed the boy to lapse into a dreamy reverie until the piano intro of "Riders on the Storm" rippled from the speakers. He still did not open his eyes until Morrison's voice did not come bursting into the mix where it should have. It was as if someone had erased the vocal track from a song Frederick had heard hundreds of times before.

Bobby propped himself up on one elbow and stared through the eerie glow of the black light posters at his turntable. It was a Dual of the latest design and was equipped with a dust cover made of smoked plastic. Rising from the spinning disc beneath was a human head.

The face stopped rotating and became more distinct. It completely filled the space beneath the dust cover. The "Riders on the Storm" instrumental track continued to play as Bobby blinked in disbelief at the oh-too-familiar shock of brown hair and vacant, bulging eyes. The other features were as youthful and angelic as they had looked in 1967.

"Jim! Jim!" Bobbie gasped.

"It's hip here, man," replied the face after a moment.

"W-w-where are you? You're supposed to be d-d-dead or. . .in Africa."

"On the other side of morning. . ."

"The. . .what?"

"Don't have to put up with a bunch of bullshit here, man. Don't have to stay loaded to make the scene. No hang-ups about sex, nakedness. . ."

"What about parents?"

"My old man, the admiral, would never make it here. Yours either. Dig?"

Suddenly, the pounding on the bedroom door grew louder and more insistent. Each rap was punctuated with the incoherent raging of Bobby's father. In a daze the boy rose to his feet. Lurching toward his turntable, he muttered, "Jim. Jim! Can you give me sanctuary, Jim?"

"Sure, man. . .Just lift the dust cover. . .I'll help ya, man."

As Bobby approached his stereo, the music engulfed him. It took all of his strength to obey his shaman's command. Then, it was as if Morrison's voice echoed from the boy's own being. He never heard his father kick in the bedroom door. He stood transfixed, humming madly, watching the Elektra butterfly on the record label spin around and around. . .

THE ONE AND ONLY PRICE VINCENT

The guitarist bent scowling over his instrument. He had stayed up all night to compose a song, and it was easy to tell by the sullenness of his eyes that he was far from satisfied with the results. As he strummed the catchy chords over and over, his mind fumbled vaguely for suitable lyrics.

Just as the guitarist was about to give up in frustration, the front door swung open and in strode a hip, bearded young man with several sheets of typing paper clutched tightly in his hand. With him from the street, he brought the echoes of a waking city pulsing into life.

"What's shakin', dude?" asked the visitor. "Hey, that sounds like a really happenin' tune you're workin' on."

"Yeah, Willard," grunted the guitarist with a thin smile. "It's gonna be a million-seller. I just know it."

"You've hit on a good riff, all right. Say, if you haven't got any lyrics yet, why don't you take a look at these, Price? I like wrote all five of them last night before I crashed out. Talk about a creative burst!"

Willard perched on a stool next to Price Vincent and handed him the neatly typed lyric sheets he had gotten up early to prepare. With surprise he noted the hard look that passed over the guitarist's face when he snatched them up.

"Hey, Price, just from the portion of your song I overheard, I'm sure the words to my 'Hannah' will fit it perfectly. Check it out, dude!"

Vincent leafed through the pages until he found the lyrics Willard was so enthused about. Halfheartedly, he skimmed through them before tossing aside his partner's work. As the lyric sheets rained to the floor, he sprang from his stool and slammed his instrument in its case. He was careful Willard did not see the jealous hatred burning in his eyes when he bolted for the control room.

After Price had stomped away, Willard snatched up one of the scattered sheets and followed after him. "Hey, you didn't tell me what you thought of 'Hannah,' " he blared, laying his lyric on the control board where the musician would be sure to see it. "If you don't like that one, I'll be glad to help you revise whatever you've started."

"Don't be so damn pushy!" snapped Vincent. "I'm nearly finished, and I don't need *your* help!"

"Hey, what's wrong with you lately, man? It seems like every time I make a suggestion, you snap my head off."

"Don't you think I'm capable of writing my own lyrics? Didn't I compose the band's first big hit, 'Rivers of Blood?' "

Willard leaned against a filing cabinet and stared hard at his friend, who hovered over the control board with his back toward him. Price's shoulder-length hair concealed the sides of his face, shielding the dark thoughts that lurked there.

"Hey, why won't you work with me anymore?" squeaked the lyricist. "I wrote over fifty lyrics in the past six months, and you've used only one of them."

To emphasize his point, Willard jerked open the bottom drawer of the filing cabinet and revealed a veritable treasure trove of his material. "Why do you think I've penned all these? For the sake of mental exercise? Look at me, man!"

Price mumbled something under his breath but did not turn around.

"Man, you know I write topnotch stuff! After all, haven't I won prizes for my work in international competitions? Haven't I?"

The guitarist stiffened at his partner's crowing. Willard had been bragging about those prizes for months. In an effort to keep his cool, Vincent snatched up a screwdriver and began drumming it against the face of the control board. *If only Willard would shut up,* he thought. *I'm much too tired to deal with this hassle now. I need sleep, bad. I–*

"Price, I need to know now! When do you plan to start using my material again? Don't forget that I've been doing the grunt work for you and the Electrocutioners for like eight years. Yeah, from the beginning I've been your lyricist, roadie, and publicity agent. Now, that we're on the verge of stardom, it seems like a poor time to cut me out. Sure your one song was our first hit single, but you don't have to be greedy. How do you expect me to benefit financially if you don't release any of my material? After all the hard work I put into this band, I deserve better!"

The guitarist still did not answer. Instead, he surveyed the outer studio through the Plexiglas window above the control board. As he noted the stack of amplifiers piled next to the front door in readiness for that night's gig, he thought about how much sweat and money he himself had funneled into the band. Had he not taken out personal loans for the equipment truck, PA system, and studio recording deck? Had he not—

"Hey, Price, hey! Answer me!" shouted Willard into his partner's ear. He was now so furious that his voice rose to a piercing, obnoxious pitch. There was also a nasty gleam in his eyes as he continued: "Price, if you're not reasonable about this, I'm left with no alternative. You know how the copyright forms include each author and his contribution? Well, if you remember, we weren't required to tell which individual songs were co-written and which were not. That means that as far as the boys in Washington are concerned, I helped you with every single tune on our last copyright tape. Yeah, I'm gonna swear I'm the co-author even if you did write all but one song yourself. Dig?"

Price's eyes widened in acknowledgment. "Like hell!" he roared, turning to bury the screwdriver he had been fingering into his partner's throat.

Surprise gurgled from Willard's crushed voice box. Then, he toppled backward, blood spurting from the hole in his larynx. With his last gasp of breath he watched horrified as Price grabbed "Hannah" from the control board and torched it with a lighter.

A vicious leer burned on Vincent's face while he watched the typed lyrics sheet burn down to his fingertips. He dropped the charred embers to the floor and furiously stomped them out. Then, he glanced madly about the studio, chanting, "What to do with the body? The body. The body. What to do with the body? Now, that I freed its dark soul! Why, that's it. The lyrics I searched for all night! Yeah, what can I do with you Willard? Now, that I freed your black soul. . ."

It was minutes before show time, and electricity surged through the air. While Price adjusted his guitar strap, he glanced across the darkened stage toward the shadowy figures of roadies who scurried back and forth moving monitors and setting up mike stands. Red amplifier eyes and lit cigarettes glowed in the murk. Although Price couldn't distinguish his drummer, he knew that he was behind his kit by the tattoo of drum sticks rattling from snare to tom to cymbal and back again. As he listened to the primal beat, he quivered with the excitement felt by boxers before a championship bout. After all, wasn't performing life's ultimate high?

When two shadows glided toward their microphones to Price's right, he strode to his amplifier and plugged in his guitar. At that moment the audience flickered with the gleam of a thousand lighters held head-high by the impatient crowd. He was about to join his bassist center stage when the head roadie grabbed him by the arm and whispered, "Hey, Price, have you seen Willard? He was supposed to run the follow spot tonight."

"Yeah, he's around here somewhere, but I don't think he'll be of much help."

"Why not?"

"He's been having some trouble with his throat."

"What does that have to do with him helping with the light show?" grumbled the roadie.

"Hey, that's not my problem! Do the best you can!" snarled Vincent as he shook himself free from the other's grasp. "Willard may show up later, but I doubt it."

Before the roadie could protest further, there was a blinding burst of light. Flashpots exploding near the front of the stage bathed the band in eerie crimson. The kids in the audience squealed with unbridled delight when the M.C. shouted above the din, "Ladies and gentlemen, it is with great pleasure that on behalf of the Fairfield College student government, I present the one and only Price Vincent and the Electrocutioners!"

Right on cue, Price leaped into the spotlight that appeared center stage. Cranking his guitar to five, he laid down some nasty licks. With the rest of band blasting away behind him, he danced and gyrated like a madman undergoing electroshock therapy. He did a split at the exact moment the stage again exploded with flashpot fire.

The louder the audience howled its approval, the louder Vincent cranked his guitar. By midway through the set, he had the dial turned to eight as he boogied through a Rolling Stone oldie, "Satisfaction." He and his bassist bumped to the beat while pumping their instruments in a suggestive fashion. When the rhythm section settled into a pulsing groove, Price screamed into the microphone, "Have any of you people ever loved someone who wouldn't even fart in your face? Well, I have!"

"Me, too," chirped the bassist, "and it ain't no fun!"

"Well, what can a dude do about it?" growled Price. "You don't know? Well, let me tell ya! When your baby don't wantcha, you gotta do what ya gotta do. Know what that is?"

"No-o-o-o!!" echoed the crowd.

"You gotta get out the Jack. The Jack Daniels. When you and he become real familiar, you gotta, you gotta walk right up to your baby. That's right! You gotta walk right up to her and say, 'BA-BYYY, I WANNA JUMP YER BONES!"

There was absolute bedlam as 10,000 howling fans expressed their personal satisfaction. To compensate for the noise level, Price again adjusted the volume control on his guitar. Cranking it up to ten, he danced into the spotlight that appeared once more center stage. Windmilling his right arm, he struck five impressive chords and then raised both fists over his head in a gesture of triumph. At that exact instant, a shower of sparks erupted from Vincent's guitar, and he jerked convulsively forward, toppling over his mike stand. As he wobbled to his knees, the audience was on its feet for a rousing ovation. It wasn't until the drummer had pounced from behind his kit to unplug Price's amp that the crowd began to realize the guitarist's collapse wasn't part of the act.

Suddenly, the curtain tumbled down, and the stage was awash with roadies and security guards who gathered around Price as he writhed and contorted, near death. The head roadie even had the presence of mind to check the guitarist's amplifier. When he noticed that the back was loose, he produced a screwdriver from his pocket and removed the cover. He was greeted by a horrible stench. Gagging, he backed away in search of reinforcements. He returned with a security guard in tow, and they spun the amp farther away from the stage wall to have a look inside. Their flashlight beams revealed the charred remains of a severed human hand lodged against a shorted transformer tube.

With the stench of burnt flesh strong in his nostrils, the head roadie remembered his conversation with Price before the show. On a hunch, he stumbled over to the towering bass cabinet and pried off the cover. The security guard had gone to vomit. Maybe it was just as well he didn't stick around, for the roadie was about to discover how a simple case of throat trouble had kept Willard from his light crew duties. What no one would be able to explain was the vengeful leer that gleamed so horribly from the lyricist's decapitated head.

FETTERS AND CHAINS

Jason came from a very unloving family. Although he was an only child, his parents were usually too busy despising each other to pay him much mind. His most vivid childhood memories were of sullen faces, threatening fists, and constant bickering. It is no wonder, then, that at a very early age, Jason decided marriage was a trap to be avoided at all costs.

In accordance with this resolution, Jason spent his early teenage years avoiding the opposite sex. Sure there were moments when a hint of perfume or the curve of girlish hips would arouse in him the vague animal lust peculiar to the pubescent male. But those lapses were always short-lived, for his built-in defense mechanism would conjure pinched images of his mother's owlish face so grotesque that he would turn away in disgust from the object of his longing.

Strangely enough, it was this very aloofness that made Jason most appealing to those he sought to evade. Also, by the time he was seventeen, he had become so darkly handsome, with his flashing black eyes and chiseled features, that every girl in his class longed to be the one to unlock the mysterious brooding that possessed him.

At first, Jason was puzzled by the alluring glances of the girls who sized him up as he took his seat in science or math class. When the awful truth finally dawned on him, he reacted like all true masters of any game—he used his knowledge to conquer and destroy his opponent. Naturally, being so young, Jason saw these objectives in purely sexual terms.

So began a long string of girlfriends who he found, unwrapped, and unwound. If this description sounds a bit cold and formulaic, it was meant to be, for Jason developed a foolproof strategy of cold manipulation.

Invariably, each of Jason's encounters began when he permitted the female to make the first move. This gave his "prey" a false sense of security while, at the same time, making *him* appear vulnerable until he had gained the girl's complete trust. That usually didn't take long, considering his natural cunning and facility with the tender phrase. As one of the bereaved young ladies was to remark after his disappearance, "Jason could charm Cleopatra out of the arms of Anthony."

Another useful tactic Jason learned after two or three of these romances was to keep his woman off guard through a mixture of sweetness and cruelty. As a matter of fact, it seemed that a girl became hooked on him even sooner if he was lackadaisical about returning her phone calls or avoided her in the halls at school. It was also this same enigma that made it doubly hard for him to dispose of a lover once he had had his way with her. Each abuse he heaped upon his old love always made her want him twice as bad. Little did she understand that his strained conversation and paleness were merely manifestations of the human animal balking from a trap.

Despite all the turmoil caused by his love life, Jason's senior year in high school went very well until a couple of weeks before the prom. At the time he was "between girls" and available. He had to decide which of the host of willing beauties should be given the privilege of taking him to the dance. He had narrowed it down to a pair of luscious juniors (who had been in hot pursuit for months) when the most peculiar thing occurred one morning before homeroom.

As was his custom, Jason was strolling down the hall "taking inventory." He was so intent upon rating each girl he passed—noting her figure, face, and future possibilities—that it took him awhile to realize he, too, was under scrutiny.

Fearing that a teacher had guessed his game, he wheeled stiffly around, half expecting to discover a ferret-faced adult behind him. Instead, he found himself examining the shapeliest girl he had ever seen. Such a judgment was easy to make, considering she stood framed in a sunlit doorway which revealed every shadowy curve of her body through her dress. Ironically, the same dazzling glare that highlighted her figure also masked her cocked face in a blinding aura of amber light.

As Jason noted every delicious inch of the girl's body, he became instantly aroused. He attempted to compliment her with his old line but found his throat so unnaturally constricted that he was unable to speak. Utterly disarmed by desire, he felt almost naked himself. In fact, he was so uncomfortable that he never questioned why such a dainty girl should wear a spiked chain bracelet more befitting the Hell's Angels than a high school co-ed.

At last, the girl shot Jason a dazzling smile. Numbly, he began babbling disjointed phrases that could have made no possible sense to anyone but her. When he walked away in a daze, even he could only recall that the girl's name was Hester and that *he* had asked *her* to the prom. Although he could not distinctly recall seeing her face, it's doubtful he could have resisted anyway.

On the night of the big dance, Jason was uncharacteristically apprehensive. He stayed locked in his bedroom all evening, adjusting his tux and fussing over his appearance. Finally, with the eighth chime of the hall clock ringing in his head, he stomped downstairs to hiss goodbye to his parents. He was especially uncivil to his mother when she dropped his date's corsage while fetching it from the refrigerator. His father's joke about him looking like a "stiff in a monkey suit" went over about as well. But who were they? Let them wallow in their ugly world.

Even behind the wheel of his old man's car, Jason couldn't relax. Nothing playing on the radio satisfied him, and he skipped from station to station. He wondered why he had not seen his date since that first morning. It seemed just plain unnatural that she hadn't phoned him or, at least, waited around for him after school. Was it possible that she actually planned to stand him up? How foolish he would look if he went to the biggest social event of the year with no lady hanging on his arm!

Only visions of Hester's sweet, shadowy figure kept Jason from totally panicking as he turned onto Denison Street and speeded toward the address the girl had given him during their only encounter. Could it be that she actually lived in such a ramshackle neighborhood? Had he not been so driven by lust, he certainly wouldn't have stayed to find out once he spied her soot-blackened apartment house dwarfed by the smokestacks of a nearby meat processing plant. As it was, he barely noticed the reek of old blood from the slaughterhouse next door when he boiled from his vehicle and charged up the front steps.

With his pulse thundering in his temples, Jason tapped lightly on the front door. Although it was a muggy May night, his teeth chattered and his eyes had a vague, glazed look about them. He was forced to rap more vigorously before he heard the clatter of high heels approaching from inside.

Finally, the door creaked open, and Jason was blinded by a flash of light. Only Hester's enticing voice told him he was indeed at the right address. He did not step inside until her hot fingers closed around his wrist like a set of manacles.

When the boy's eyes had adjusted to the glare, he found himself standing in a cavernous living room, the entire back wall of which was dominated by a blazing fireplace. A mantle lined with strange, ebony curios ran the full length of this wall. Before the fireplace was a circle of furniture made of polished black oak. The chairs and settees glistened with such brilliance they appeared to generate their own light.

Then, Jason's gaze lit upon Hester where she stood with firelight dancing on her face. Her own eyes were coyly downcast, and her lips were pursed into a welcoming smile. She was attired in a black, formal gown that sparkled seductively. Its plunging neckline attracted Jason like a thief is drawn to a strand of pearls.

Sensing her advantage, Hester ensnared Jason in her arms and led him in an enchanted waltz around the chamber as soft music began to play. Jason was so bewitched by the sensual nature of this melody that he lost track of the course their dance followed across the living room and down an adjacent hallway. Then, Hester released her embrace, retreated a step, and slipped her dress off her shoulders and onto the floor. All thoughts of the prom slipped from Jason's mind, as well.

Jason blinked in amazement as he drank in every slinky curve of the girl's naked form. At last, he realized they were in a dimly-lit bedroom, and that she was motioning for him to lie back on the water bed behind him. When she saw he was too numb to respond, she took his hand and ran it across the satin coverlet over the bed. This simple act brought him unspeakable pleasure and promised even more.

With the recklessness only carnal lust can produce, Jason tumbled backward and reached out his hand for his lover. He hit the coverlet with a sploosh that made the gooseflesh thick on his buttocks. The next instant he felt himself sinking out of sight in a benumbing tank of dark liquid. He was completely out of breath by the time he touched the bottom, shoved off with one foot, and propelled himself to the surface. When he broke water, he was greeted by his first real glimpse of Hester's eyes.

A scream rattled from Jason's throat, and he sank from sight a second time. With the freezing water deadening his limbs, it felt like an eternity before he again hit bottom. When his left foot finally did touch, a pair of jaws clamped shut around his ankle. Sharp teeth tore at his flesh, and a cloud of blood bubbled upward past his face. In an animal frenzy Jason kicked and thrashed until the lack of oxygen choked the fight out of him. Only as his tuxedo-clad form sagged to the bottom of the tank, did he see the bear trap that secured him.

Meanwhile, two crimson pupils peered expectantly downward into the dank pool. Just as the water quit bubbling, the faint buzz of a doorbell echoed from down the hall. Hester glanced once more into the water to note a second trap and then pulled the satin coverlet in place over the bed frame. As she left the room, her hellish eyes were cast coyly downward. Her formal gown glistened with every delicious movement of her hips.

NORTH HALL IS HAUNTED

"They don't call Mansfield a suitcase college for nothing," grumbled Susan, watching her roommate hurry to pack her clothes.

"What's a girl to do?" replied Sherry. "This campus is so dead on weekends that it's just not worth staying here. Why don't you split, too?"

"My parents won't allow it. They say they're paying good money for me to have 'the total college experience,' which doesn't include running back to *their* house all the time. My father even wants me to sign up for the summer semester."

"Then, why don't you visit your Aunt Celia? You're always talking about her. I remember how cool she was at orientation."

"My aunt's special all right. I don't think I'd have gotten through adolescence without her helping me with my problems. But she already invited me for Thanksgiving. I'd hate to impose on her now. She's so busy running her flower shop."

"Well, you could get yourself a boyfriend, Sooze. That'd keep you occupied."

"You know as well as I do that the boys on this campus are pigs. All they do is brag about their sexual adventures. You've heard them! They don't want a serious relationship with a girl. Jerks like that are only interested in one thing."

65

"But if you got interested in it, too," giggled Sherry, "you wouldn't have to worry about being bored. That's why they keep the TV lounge so dark, you know."

"I'd rather study until my eyeballs fall out than go to the Passion Pit with some hogman. I know what goes on there."

"Then, what are you going to do for two whole days?"

"Work on my psych report, I guess. I'm assigned one every month. There sure won't be any noise to distract me with everyone else on our floor leaving."

"Aren't you scared to stay here by yourself after all the stories flying around this week about the ghost?"

"What stories?" asked Susan.

"Boy, you do study too much! The way I heard it, Debbie Weaver went up to practice on the piano in the attic. As she climbed the stairs, she heard someone playing an old ragtime song."

"What's so spooky about that?"

"When Debbie opened the attic door, the music just stopped. And there was nobody sitting at the piano."

"That's creepy all right."

"What's creepy?" asked a surly girl after banging open Susan's door with an overnight bag. "Hurry up, Sherry. We don't want to miss our bus. My Delta Zeta sisters have already left for the terminal and will save us a good seat. I sure hope you pledge our sorority. We'll all love having you as a member."

"I'm almost finished, Barbara. I was just telling Susan about the North Hall ghost."

"The one Debbie heard?"

"You mean you also know about the spook?" asked Susan with a look of trepidation.

"Sure!" replied Barbara, pulling a red beret over her silky hair. "You must be from Mars if you don't know about *her*."

"Her?"

"Yeah, your dorm has been haunted since World War I. My sorority sister told me the story months ago. It seems this lovesick girl got really freaked out after her boyfriend was killed in the trenches of France. She started fooling around with a Ouija board and did all sorts of strange stuff trying desperately to contact him. Her parents, the housemother, and a psychiatrist all counseled her, but she wouldn't listen. One night, after consulting the spirits, she ran screaming out into the hall and leaped down the stairwell. She fell six flights to the cafeteria in the basement where a security guard found her bloody, dead body. Every freshman class since then has seen her ghost roaming North Hall. And she lived right on this floor!"

"I guess I better keep my Ouija board in the closet, then," tittered Sherry. "I wouldn't want to rile up the spirit world."

"Or your spooked roomie, either," sneered Barbara, noting the hollow look in Susan's eyes.

"Hey, we gotta go, Sooze. See you Sunday night if you haven't shacked up with a cute boy by then."

"Or lapsed into a coma is more like it," mocked Barbara with obvious disdain.

"Get outta here!"

Waving goodbye, Sherry and Barbara shot out the door and merged with a constant stream of freshmen coeds making for the stairwell. The exodus continued for another hour until the sounds of hurried footsteps, swishing skirts, and happy giggles were replaced by a deep, pervading silence.

To escape the ominous hush, Susan closed her door and turned on the radio. The only station that came in clearly was WNTE broadcast by the college. WNTE played a mix of Top 40 hits, and the girl plopped in front of the mirror to brush her hair and sing along to the Beach Boys. "We'll have fun, fun, fun!" she chirped in a breathy alto. "Yeah, right!"

Susan examined her oval face and full lips in the mirror. *Why couldn't I get a boyfriend?* she wondered. *I'm just as cute as Sherry. She's not kidding me. The "real" reason she goes home every weekend is to see that guy Steven she moans about in her sleep. I got nice, long hair that flips up on the end. And straight teeth, too. But why did I have to be born a dumb, old redhead? Everyone knows we're all. . .so temperamental. . .*

A sudden knock startled Susan from her reverie, and she leaped up to face the door. "W-w-who is it?" she stammered. "W-w-what do you want?"

"It's Mrs. Phillips. I need to talk with you."

Susan scurried to the door to admit a tall, brisk woman in her late 50's who served as housemother of North Hall. The lady stepped inside, and despite herself, checked the neatness of the room before saying, "Sherry Morgan just stopped by my office. Like any good resident assistant, she was worried about leaving you up here all alone. Are you going to be okay staying on this deserted floor by yourself? I have a spare bedroom in my suite downstairs if you'd like to room with me this weekend."

"Oh, Sherry shouldn't have bothered you. I'm fine," assured the redhead, imagining the ribbing she'd get from Barbara should she accept this offer. "I'm used to being alone. It's not a problem."

"Are you sure?" asked Mrs. Phillips, noting the strain in Susan's voice.

"Sure!"

"Oh, and I brought you a package."

"Thank you! Why, it's from Aunt Celia!"

"She sends these quite often, doesn't she?"

"Yes. She's my lifeline to the outside world."

"Then, it must be a care package, dear," replied the housemother with a comforting smile. "Would you like me to walk you down to dinner?"

"Okay. I could try to eat something."

"Be sure to lock your door!"

Susan turned off her radio. Then, she slipped on her tennis shoes and followed Mrs. Phillips down six flights of stairs to the basement cafeteria. There was no activity on any of the floors they passed on the way. The café was nearly deserted, as well, when the girl bid the housemother "good evening" and joined a short line of athletes who were also stuck on campus.

After filling up her tray, Susan sat by herself in a corner watching the football players wolf down steaming plates of spaghetti. Ever since she had arrived two months ago, the girl had practically lived on milk. Everything else she found undercooked or burnt to a crisp by the Mansfield food service. Not that her mother's cooking was much better.

Susan glanced down at her tray and frowned in disbelief. "The cooks can even ruin Jello!" she muttered. "Yuck! They put onions in it. Those meatheads on the football team must be getting special food. How do they get their necks so thick? They can't even look sideways anymore! Not that they'd notice me, anyway."

Susan nibbled on a piece of Italian bread smeared with rancid butter that made her gag. With a disgusted frown, she picked up her fork and took a bite of salad tainted with hated radishes. When the spaghetti was too soggy to stomach, she leaped up and dumped the contents of her tray, dishes and all, into the trash bin.

In a huff, the girl stormed outside. She ran down the sidewalk into a wooded park that stretched down the hill in front of her dorm. "My parents must really hate me to have talked me into coming here," she groaned, collapsing on a wooden bench. "So what if Father and Granddad are in the Mansfield State College Jock Hall of Fame? They were too busy scoring goals and kicking home runs to worry about being stuck in the middle of Pennsylvania's boondocks. The jocks aren't the only animals on this campus. We also have skunks, rabbits, and squirrels."

Susan burst into tears as she glanced at North Hall, the foreboding Gothic building that dominated the center of campus. "I hate my dorm," she bawled. "The towers are straight out of a Vincent Price movie. It's a wonder those windows don't have bars on them. And look at that ugly red brick. I swear this place would make a great sanitarium."

The girl covered her face with her hands and continued to sob until the long shadow cast by North Hall engulfed her. The sun was close to setting, and a few gray squirrels ran from the trees to dig for acorns before darkness fell. Their chattering roused Susan from her self-pity, and she became aware of a bitter cold that had invaded the late evening air. Shivering, she rose from the bench and trudged dejectedly up the hill toward the cafeteria door.

Back in her room, Susan resumed her disheartening conversation with herself. "I wish I was more like Sherry," she murmured. "She always knows the right thing to say. Everyone loves her to pieces even though she is a tough floor monitor. If she hadn't taken me in after the fight I had with my three roommates on second floor, I would have quit college for sure. I just couldn't deal with sharing a room with that many girls after being an only child. I still can't believe Sherry let a loser like me stay in her R.A. suite."

Susan picked up her psychology text and leafed through it with disinterest. "It's a wonder my case history isn't written up in here," whimpered the coed. "The chapter title could read, 'The Invisible Girl.' That's me. It's like I never existed in high school. I had no dates, no club invitations, no one to notice.

"Even my parents didn't care if I ever left my room. They were too busy sleeping around to pay me much mind. Yeah, they fancied themselves quite the swingers. The way Father strutted around in his smoking jacket, you'd think he was Hugh Hefner. He didn't fool me any. Even a big executive like him couldn't have had *that* many secretaries. And Mother was just as bad. Every Saturday night she left the house dressed like Zsa Zsa Gabor. When she finally did stagger home, she always reeked of alcohol and strange men's cologne. Eeewww!

"And now that backstabbing Barbara wants to steal my only friend at MSC. I hate that snob. All she talks about is being a Delta Zeta. If she gets Sherry to join her little clique, I might as well *be* the North Hall ghost."

The girl slammed down her book and stared bitterly out the dorm window. The lights of the other dormitories glowed eerily through a dense fog that wrapped itself around the hillside campus. Braying laughter floated from the sidewalk below as a few nerds spilled from the closing library across the lane. "I'm so pathetic, I don't even fit in with those kids," sighed Susan. "I guess I'll go to bed. . ."

The redhead had just changed into her pajamas when she heard footsteps tramp deliberately up the stairwell and move to the far end of the hall. *That,* thought the coed, *must be one-armed Lefty, the dumb, old security guard, making his rounds. Like he could do anything if there was trouble.*

Susan listened intently as the visitor halted before a distant door and knocked twice. After unlocking and opening the door, the visitor closed it again and moved on to the next room. Methodically, the doors opened and closed all down the hall until the footsteps were even with her chamber. Instead of the expected knock, the caller moved past to check the rest of the vacant sixth floor.

Must have seen the light shining under my door, reasoned Susan after the visitor strode by. *Maybe I'd better see who's out there. . .*

Working up her courage, the girl slipped on a pink bathrobe and a pair of bunny slippers. Then, she crept toward the door and grabbed the knob. The footsteps continued to grow fainter as she fumbled with the lock. By the time she peeped into the hall, the visitor had moved even with the stairwell.

Instead of old Lefty, there floated a misty figure in a baggy-sleeved dress. Her abundant hair was straight on top and curly down the back of her neck. She wore high-topped shoes and dark stockings. Turning, she fixed Susan with a peaceful, dreamy smile. She opened her arms and beckoned with both hands before slowly fading from view.

With a gasp, Susan slammed her door and fought to lock it behind her. "A lot of good this will do," she muttered, "when the ghost has the floor key! Why didn't I accept Mrs. Phillips' offer? Damn my pride, anyway. I get that from Father, the pig."

The girl nervously brushed a stray strand of hair away from her face and then scrambled to turn on her study light. For good measure, she snapped on her roommate's lamp, too. Snatching her Bible from a shelf, Susan withdrew a crucifix Aunt Celia had given her as a confirmation gift and placed it in the breast pocket of her bathrobe. Finally, she collapsed on the bed to think things through.

"It figures that I'd be the one the ghost appears to," ranted the coed. "Scary old Susan, spirit's friend. Too spooky for this world. Too weird to fit in. Thank God for the time I spent with Aunt Celia. She's the only loving person in my whole damn family. Why, I better open that package she sent me. Oh, look! She remembered how much I love chocolate chip cookies. Awww! A photo of her and me at the Thousand Islands, New York. We had such fun on that vacation. We shopped, swam, and took the boat tour. Why couldn't Celia have been my mother? She has respect for my feelings. *She wouldn't have sent me to this spooky, old college.*"

Bursting into tears, Susan buried her head in her pillow. After she had cried herself out, she sat up and blew her nose.

"M-m-maybe, I should see what the ghost wanted," mumbled the girl. "Didn't prissy Barbara say a Ouija board lets you communicate with the spirit world? Duh! I should know that. I just wrote a paper for psych class on Ouija boards. I even examined the one Sherry has in her closet while I was doing my research. There. I see it."

Susan crossed the floor and snatched the Ouija board from the top shelf of her roommate's meticulously organized wardrobe. With trembling hands, she pulled it out of the box and laid it on her desk. The board had a smiling sun painted in the top left corner with the word "Yes" next to it. In the top right corner was a frowning moon with "No" beside it.

The sun represents the God of the Spirit World, remembered Susan from her report. *The quarter phase moon stands for the Goddess of the Spirit World.*

Below the two images was the word "OUIJA" printed in bold letters and centered on the board. Under that, all the letters of the alphabet were stretched out in two rows from *A* to *Z*. A row of numbers from 1 to 0 came next. At the very bottom of the board Susan found the words "GOOD BYE."

My professor warned against using the board when I chose this topic, reflected the girl, tugging tentatively on her long hair. *I even listened to him. But that was. . .before.*

Even if spirit channeling is a dangerous business, I just gotta try to reach. . .that ghost. She seemed so happy. Something I want to be. Maybe. . .she. . .can help me. She couldn't be an evil presence, the way she was smiling. . .

Susan picked up the wooden planchette and laid it on the board. The planchette was heart-shaped and had three felt-tipped legs that facilitated its movement. In the center was a plastic window to peer through.

Susan placed her right hand on the planchette. As she deliberately began circling the board with it, she asked politely, "Did I see the North Hall ghost?"

Susan pressed a little harder on the Message Indicator. She moved it faster. Suddenly, the lights began to flicker. A hair brush floated from the girl's dresser and hovered in the air. The girl screamed and let go of the planchette. Her hand no sooner sprang from the heart-shaped object when it moved on its own and spelled out the letters *YES.*

"W-w-why did you visit me?" stuttered the girl as the brush flew into her hand.

I FELT YOUR PAIN, answered the planchette.

As Susan read the message, the bulb in her roommate's study lamp flashed wickedly and blew out. Then, her psychology text lifted from the desk and began circling her head. Its movement had a hypnotic effect on her, and she asked numbly, "What should I do?"

The textbook dropped into Susan's lap and flew open to the chapter dealing with suicide. Afterward, the planchette moved slowly and deliberately to spell *JUMP.*

A smile played across Susan's lips. She rose from the bed. Walking mechanically to the door, she turned the lock. The door creaked open of its own accord. She stepped into the hall. There, a sudden gust of cold wind mussed her hair and numbed her paling cheeks. She strode transfixed toward a wispy figure standing atop the stairwell railing. The figure smiled invitingly and held out her arms in a gesture of love.

Just before Susan reached the beckoning spirit, a second blast of wind blew her hair across her eyes. When she reached to clear her face, her hand brushed against the crucifix in her breast pocket. The holy cross felt warm to her touch, and she could feel her heartbeat pulsing through it. Images of her dear Aunt Celia popped into her brain with sun-filled afternoons and tall glasses of delicious lemonade.

With a shake of her head, Susan cleared the strands of hair blocking her vision. Clutching the crucifix, she saw the ghost's sweet smile twist into a malicious leer. An expression of self-loathing and total despair revealed the fate that doomed her soul in 1917.

"The damned aren't happy!" cried Susan. "In the name of Jesus Christ, get away from me!"

With a fearful gasp, the ghost recoiled at the holy name. Before Susan could again say "Jesus Christ," the figure lunged forward to snare the coed in its lethal arms. Susan dodged and bolted for the stairwell. In the next instant she was sprinting toward the fifth floor. No lights came on there in response to her cries for help, so she scrambled down and down into the bowels of North Hall. Blindly she ran with a cold wind shrieking at her heels, trying to capsize her. Only her instincts and awakened will allowed her to keep her balance as the wind buffeted her from behind.

Susan descended to the cafeteria just as her churning legs turned to rubber. She no sooner stumbled into the murky room when a hellish, disappointed wail filled the stairwell behind her. The cold, pursuing wind came to a sudden halt and then sucked upward floor by floor until it vanished in the direction of the attic.

With the last of her strength, Susan crossed the cafeteria, pushed through the hallway doors, and staggered past the vacant TV lounge to Mrs. Phillips' suite. Fighting back the blackness closing around her, she rapped desperately on the smiley face taped to the housemother's door.

The terrified girl tottered at the threshold until a very sleepy Mrs. Phillips answered her flurry of knocks. "I couldn't jump! Couldn't jump!" babbled the coed, collapsing into the housemother's arms. "Help me. Please! Help me live. I want so much to. . .live. To thank Aunt Celia for her. . .love. . ."

ESTRANGED

Charlie Watson emerged from a heavy sleep. A faint buzz, he recognized as a rattler's warning, pricked his senses and brought his brain to full alert. Cautiously, he opened his eyes as sweat popped on his brow and his pulse pounded with fear. Glancing warily about, he searched for the fang-bared reptile that must have crawled through the torn screen door of his Florida bungalow. He moved his hand an inch at a time until it touched the handle of his nightstand drawer where he stashed his pistol. It wasn't until he had eked the drawer half open that he realized that the saurian buzzing came from his telephone.

With a shiver, Watson snatched up the receiver and grunted, "Hello?"

"Is that you, Charlie?"

"I'm the only one living here. Of all people, you should know that, Lauren."

"Just because we're separated, you don't have to be nasty," replied a silky voice.

"What do you want?"

"Well, I'm down at the airport and need a lift to your mother's house. I didn't think it would be proper if I stayed with you. . .until we patch up our differences."

"At my mother's?" gasped Charlie. "Does she know you're coming?"

"Of course, silly. I called her from Chicago last week."

"And she agreed to let you in her house?"

"She still loves me, Charlie, even if you don't. Why, you make me sound like some kind of monster."

"Aren't you?"

"Won't you come pick me up? P-p-please?"

"But I just pulled a double shift at the knife factory, Lauren. Why can't you take a cab?"

"Same old Charlie. Gone from an alcoholic to a workaholic just like that! If you ever cared for me even a little, you gotta come down. I-I-I-I don't have money for a taxi."

"All right! Give me an hour. What time is it, anyway?"

"Noon."

Watson slammed down the receiver, crawled groggily to his feet, and pulled on a rumpled pair of work pants. After slugging down two cups of coffee, he washed his face and ran a comb through his thick, iron-colored hair. He hardly recognized the wrecked visage that stared back at him from the mirror. Five years of ceaseless toil had eroded deep creases in his forehead and turned his eyes into listless pools of sludge. Even his Sundays were no fun. That was when he did his laundry, cleaned his house, and helped his widowed mother with her bills and chores.

"It's like I've been working on a chain gang since Lauren and I became estranged," muttered Charlie. "I'd like to move. Start over again. But then what would poor Mother do? She's such a kind person, she'd see the good in Jeffrey Dahmer! My shrink would call her an 'enabler.' I just wish Mom would see Lauren for the conniving bitch she is."

Charlie banged shut the door behind him but didn't bother to lock it. Except for the pistol, he knew there was nothing worth stealing in the whole house. He had no television or stereo. His refrigerator leaked Freon. The stove had a sprung oven door. All his furniture was secondhand.

"Why in the hell did Lauren have to come back?" puzzled Watson. "She kills everything she touches, man. Every nerve, every heart, every soul! Now, she's gonna screw up my only working relationship — the one with my mother."

Charlie crawled behind the wheel of his VW Bug and bounced down the one-lane track through the Glades he called home. Often, he had to stop and let gators slither off the road. Exotic birds, plumed in bright blues and greens, squawked at his intrusion, while rabbits fled into the brush on every straightaway. Haunted by scary flashbacks of his marriage to Lauren, he finally arrived at the highway after four bumpy miles.

Charlie's alertness increased as the traffic grew heavier with each mile he sped toward Miami. Soon, he was weaving in and out of a constant flow of passenger cars, SUVs, and oversized tractor trailers. After swearing at an obnoxious trucker that swerved in front of him each time he tried to pass, he glanced fuming out the window at the squat, stucco dwellings lining the Tamiami Trail.

"Look at the bars on those windows," he grunted. "And they're in the houses. I may be imprisoned by my work, but at least I don't *live* in jail."

Watson cut off a honking tourist and veered into the Miami International Airport. He hated the bustle of the place and the deafening roar of airliners as they took off or landed. After screeching into a parking spot, he locked his car and shifted his wallet to his front pocket. He was carrying a week's salary for his mortgage payment and didn't need to be mugged by the Cuban greasers that frequented the corridors and restrooms. Somehow, the lock blade knife he always carried in his pocket didn't seem enough protection here, even in the daytime. To avoid the dangerous commodes, he pissed behind a Dodge Caravan before entering the air-conditioned terminal.

Near the service desk stood a willowy redhead dressed in a tasteful blue skirt and dark blue stockings. Her hair was tied into a bun favored by the professional women of South Florida. She puffed casually on a cigarette that protruded from full, vermilion lips. She had an actress' cheekbones and nose, and would have been described as beautiful, if not for the age lines that even a heavy coat of makeup couldn't hide. When she spotted Charlie pushing through the crowd, she waved and rushed to give him a stiff hug.

"I-I-I thought you weren't coming," said Lauren with a hurt whimper. "I told your mother we'd be arriving around two. It's almost two-thirty now! You know how Clara values punctuality."

"It's not that far to Hallandale," reminded Charlie gruffly. "We'll be there soon enough without your nagging."

"I'm only thinking of your mother. At least *she'll* be happy to see me."

"And it looks like you're planning to stay with her quite a while," Watson grumbled as he struggled with two oversized suitcases. "You'll have to carry the smaller bags yourself."

Charlie broke trail through a jostling crowd surging for the exits. Using one of his wife's suitcases, he smacked open a terminal door and led her on through the congested parking lot. Twice he had to set down his burdens to ease his quivering muscles. Twice more she begged him to stop, so she could rest.

"At least no one swiped my tires this time," huffed Watson upon spotting his Volkswagen Beetle.

"That's right!" recalled Lauren. "Someone stripped our BMW the last time you picked me up here. That's when I was a buyer for Jordache, and you were a power broker. I thought you were going to blow a fuse!"

"You mean like I did when seeing you now!" snapped Charlie, slamming his wife's luggage into the trunk. "We'll squeeze the rest of your bags in the backseat. It looks like the mothers will fit."

Watson scrambled behind the wheel and reached to unlock the passenger side door. His wife had barely stowed her luggage and seated herself when he floored it. Before she could snap on her seatbelt, he squealed for the lot gate and shot into the street. After nearly sideswiping a convertible blaring rap music, he blasted up the on ramp to I-90. When his VW joined the normal ebb and flow of the northbound traffic, Lauren finally squeaked, "How long have you been Speed Racer?"

"Since I quit drinking, and my reflexes returned to normal. I drive like this to survive on roads jammed with crazy fools."

"Do you isolate yourself in the swamp to survive, too?"

"Yeah, just like you became hell on high heels!"

"What happened to us, anyway, Charlie?" asked Lauren, reaching to stroke her husband's arm.

"What didn't happen would be a better question," replied Watson stiffly. "All those lavish parties and trips to Key West we couldn't afford and the half-dozen maxed-out credit cards. Yes, and we can't forget the drinking. And the way you wrapped yourself like a snake around any fellow who looked at you in Key West and at those lavish parties. Jealousy is like poison, in case you've forgotten."

"But how about the good times?"

"In bed?"

"Yeah, you know—"

"You mean I learned!" growled Charlie, pushing away his wife's groping hand. "Wasn't there a song about using sex as a weapon? I don't know why you came back here, but I won't be included in your games."

The ride to Hallandale was a silent one after Charlie's outburst. Watson kept his eyes peeled on the highway as he wove in and out of traffic with precise spurts of speed. Lauren, meanwhile, stared out the window at the distant beach. Her face was perfectly serene as if she were riding with a beloved husband who always obeyed the speed limit.

Finally, the VW swerved into the right lane and swooped onto a street heading due east. The car hadn't gone more than a couple of blocks before it wheeled left up a circular drive and screeched to a stop before a tile-roofed house set in the midst of a manicured lawn. The front door flew open and out rushed a fragile, elderly woman dressed in dirty-kneed khaki pants and a straw hat. Lauren exploded from the VW to greet her, and the two hugged like long-lost sisters.

"Well, Mother, it looks like you and Lauren have a lot of catching up to do," muttered Charlie, dumping his estranged wife's luggage on the front stoop. "I guess I better shove off."

"Aren't you at least going to stay long enough to cart in dear Lauren's things?" chided Clara Watson, wagging a bony finger at her son.

"Sorry, Mom. My shift starts at the plant in a half-hour, so I really need to get going. I see you're in your work clothes. Can't you help her?"

"Well, at least now I won't have to depend on *you* to drive me around!" snapped Clara. "Lauren will have full use of the family Oldsmobile."

"You should have learned to drive yourself after Dad died. Then, you wouldn't need to rely on anyone."

"And become a hermit like you, Son? Show some respect! Will I be seeing you Sunday?"

"Yeah, the Sunday Lauren leaves," replied Charlie, giving his mom a quick hug. "I think it best I stay away, knowing how my arguing with Lauren upsets you. Call me if you need anything."

Charlie floated in a very dark place where the sky and ocean were the exact same temperature and hue. Rollers crashed on a distant beach, and the haunted shriek of gulls echoed from a fog bank. The fin of a great shark cut the water just behind him and immediately submerged. Charlie began swimming for all he was worth. No matter how fast his legs kicked, he could feel an evil presence closing on him. He thrashed his arms and dug his hands in the churning sea until a shadow shot past him. He fought through a turbulence of bubbles and discovered the predator loomed directly in his path. It was long and sleek and deadly with a slashing, triangular tail. A mouth full of razor teeth glittered in its bullet head. With a menacing swirl, it dove at him. Closer and closer it charged until

Watson found himself staring into the cold, glittery, unmistakable eyes of Lauren.

Charlie screamed and sat straight up in bed. In his ears echoed a sharp bleat that he eventually recognized as the telephone. The sound stalled after ten rings and then started over again. It wasn't until the third sequence of rings that the trembling man grabbed the receiver and croaked, "Hello?"

"Charlie! This is your mother," squawked a frightened voice. "You need to come over here right away!"

"Over where?"

"To my house, you ninny!"

"What's wrong?"

"It's Lauren. Her pulse is irregular. She's hyperventilating. And falling all over the place—"

"Like a drunk?"

"W-w-well, yes. And I can't. . .control her. I'm afraid she'll hurt herself."

"Why don't you call 911?"

"Oh, Charlie! What would the neighbors think? You come quick! You hear?"

There was a click on the line followed by a droning dial tone. Still shaking from his dream, Charlie raced out to his car and screeched off through the night. When he arrived in Hallandale and whipped up his mother's drive, every window of her house was ablaze with light. Not bothering to knock, he bolted inside and found his mother bawling on the living room sofa. Just then, Lauren staggered up the hall dressed in a provocative nightie. With glittering eyes, she leered at him before falling flat on her face.

Charlie dragged his wife roughly to her feet. She clung to him, cooing madly, pressing her half-bared breasts against him. Then, she produced some matches and a pack of Kools from her bosom. She lit a cigarette and tossed the still burning match on the rug. As Watson leaped to stomp it out with his work boots, Lauren cackled and fell hard on her backside. She smacked against a table, upending a treasured family vase full of fresh-cut flowers. Before Clara could grab it, the vase toppled to the floor to shatter into a thousand knife-like shards. Lauren laughed again and rose to totter through the destruction, cutting her bare feet to ribbons. Before she could do any more damage to herself or the house, Charlie swept her into his arms and whisked her out to the VW. His mother, toting Lauren's bathrobe, loped behind them and crawled blubbering into the backseat.

"What's wrong with her?" cried Mrs. Watson, placing the bathrobe around her daughter-in-law's shoulders. "We've gotten along so well this past month—until tonight."

"She fell off the wagon, Mother. Can't you see? I-I-I used to act like this, too. Until I quit boozing. Watching Lauren's antics cured me. If only *she* could see how she acts when toasted!"

"But I didn't smell anything on her breath. And she's been going to AA meetings faithfully every night. Why, the day she arrived, she told me all about her battles with alcohol."

"Vodka doesn't have an odor. I've watched this drama a thousand times, Mother. I'm surprised she hasn't gone on Jerry Springer and performed her act for the whole damn country."

"But Lauren's been the perfect guest. She cleans the house, helps me in the garden, makes out my bills, does my banking—"

"Banking?"

"Why, yes. She even had the forethought of having my money put in both your names in case something should happen to me."

"Both our names?"

"You are still married, aren't you? And she's always been like a sweet daughter from the time she came into this family. For the life of me, I can't understand why you don't work out your differences with the dear girl. I'll bet Lauren's acting this way because she loves you and wants to get your attention."

Gritting his teeth, Charlie turned into the hospital and stopped at the emergency room door. He threw Lauren over his shoulder, stomped into the waiting room, and deposited her into a padded chair. As his mother spoke to the nurse who attended the paperwork, he returned outside to park his VW. Then, he walked across the street to a sports bar where he ordered a hamburger and a Coke. "It's gonna be hours before they attend to Lauren," he muttered. "Might as well feed my face in the meantime. I'd have a real drink, but who knows where that would lead?"

Charlie plopped on a barstool and buried his head in his hands. He was already stressed to the breaking point from all the double shifts he was working and didn't need this added hassle. Since his company's business tripled after the 9/11 terrorist attack, he was ceaselessly bent over his grinding wheel putting the edge on military knife blades. Engrossed in this highly dangerous work, he never spoke to anyone or took more than the mandatory lunch break. Twice he had had near fatal accidents when knives had slipped from his cramped fingers and had whipped out the top of his machine just past his head. Chewing on his tasteless burger, he almost wished they'd hit him and ended the disaster of his life.

As dawn crept into the sports bar window, Charlie rose from his stool, strode to a pay phone, and wrangled with his employer until he got the day off. Afterward, he crossed the street to find his mother sitting alone behind the drawn curtains of a room on the first floor. "Where's Lauren?" he mumbled. "Off for tests, I suppose."

"No, she ducked out the side door—to smoke."

"Smoke?"

"Yeah, even after the nurse told her ten times to stay put. Why can't she be good?"

Before Charlie could answer, an attendant dressed in green scrubs led the limping Lauren into the room. "You have to sit, ma'am," he commanded, obviously annoyed.

"Whatever. . ." slurred Charlie's wife, flopping on the bed to expose her naked buttocks through the slit in her hospital gown. "Thanks, you big, strong man."

Flushing, the attendant hurried from the room. As soon as he was gone, Lauren popped up and again headed for the exit. This time, Watson leaped to block her path and wrestle her onto the bed.

"Stop it, you two!" hissed Clara, bursting into tears. "Your behavior is giving our family a black eye! I see these nurses at the market all the time. And at the bank and flower shop. Stop it, I say!"

"Stop what?" bellowed a bossy-looking RN, bursting through the curtain. "Is the Mrs. misbehaving again? Luckily, her blood work is back from the lab. You can take her home now."

"But what made her act so. . .crazy?" blubbered Clara.

"Nothing that a pot of black coffee can't cure."

"Or a good shrink," added Charlie sourly. "Get dressed, Lauren. We'll be waiting out in the hall."

Moments later, Lauren stumbled through the curtain, pulling her nightie over her head. She flashed two male attendants wheeling a gurney into an elevator and then snatched the car keys from her startled husband's hand. "I'm—gonna—drive—home," she sang in a little girl's voice. "I'm—gonna—drive—home."

Lauren shot through the emergency room and into the parking lot, oblivious to her flopping breasts and heavily bandaged feet. She sprinted for the VW Bug and ripped open the door. Charlie caught her just as she stuck the key into the ignition and fired up the engine. Leaving a deep bruise on her arm, Watson restrained his wife before she could reach for the gear shift.

"You're mean!" Lauren whined, slapping at Charlie with a flurry of limp-wristed blows.

"And you're screwed in the head!"

"But I can drive your mommy's car anytime I want," she taunted. "Anytime I want!"

A drowning woman's voice gurgled through Charlie's subconscious. It rose like bubbles from the depths of the sea, fighting through his need for sleep. The louder it gurgled, the more familiar it became. Over and over it cried his name until he broke through the surface of reality where the voice morphed into the nonstop ringing of his telephone.

"Yes," he croaked into the receiver. "What is it?"

"I'm sorry to disturb you at such a late hour, sir," intoned a rote voice, "but there's been an accident."

"Accident?"

"Involving your mother and wife."

"Car accident?"

"Yes."

"How are they?"

"It might be better if you come to the North Miami Hospital and see for yourself. Do you know where we're located, sir? Sir?"

Charlie slammed down the phone and then rooted in his nightstand drawer for his pistol. "With all those Cubans prowling about, it's not safe in that damn city after dark," he grunted, pulling the Smith & Wesson .38 from beneath a pile of rumpled handkerchiefs. "Where's my protection permit? I'll need that for sure."

Stashing his gun in his coat pocket, Charlie ran out the door and scrambled behind the wheel of his Beetle. He spun off down the road through a torrential downpour, nearly hitting a doe and two fawns that often visited him from the swamp. A possum and her litter weren't so lucky. He barely felt their thump beneath his wheels before blasting through an endless series of puddles toward the blacktop highway.

The trip to the hospital was a blur. What Charlie found inside was a nightmare. His mother lay in intensive care with her broken legs elevated and tubes running up her nose. As shadows played across her deeply bruised face, a bleeping monitor traced her battle with death. He stayed until the life ebbed out of her, and the bleeps were replaced by an awful silence.

Charlie had not thought of his estranged wife until the rushing tread of rubber soles echoed up the corridor. Feeling completely empty, he rose and staggered to the nurse's station. There, he mumbled to a woman in flowered togs, "Where can I find Lauren Watson? Is she also in intensive care?"

"No, she didn't need much treatment. Let me see. She's in Room 425. You'll be pleased to know that she only got a few cracked ribs from the horrible collision on Route One that's been all over the news. That should ease your sorrow over losing your poor mother. I just heard. I'm so sorry. . ."

"Yeah, right!"

Charlie wheeled and stormed past the busy elevator. Flying down a flight of stairs, he slammed open the fourth floor door and stalked angrily up the hall. After knocking the bedpans from a candy striper's cart, he mowed down a doctor backing from a scrub room. He saw nothing and knew nothing but the gnawing need for revenge.

When Watson stomped into Room 425, he found his wife smoking in bed. As he strode toward her, she flashed him a bright smile and purred, "Why, Charlie, you're the one who looks like he's been in an accident. Aren't you glad I'm okay?"

"You killed Mother! Don't you know that?"

"I suspected as much after watching the paramedics work on her."

"You cold-blooded bitch!"

"Oh, lighten up, husband," advised Lauren. "After we inherit all that money Clara had stashed away, you won't have to work hard ever again."

"So that's why you came back?"

"And to love you."

"Plunge me into hell, you mean!" snarled Watson, snatching up a pillow.

"What are you going to do, smother me? You don't have the balls, dear," said Lauren, flicking her cigarette ash at Charlie.

"Don't I?"

"No, all you know how to do is run away. From your feelings. From me."

"But from Mom's murder?"

"No one will believe the wreck wasn't an accident, Daddy," cooed Lauren, slipping into her little girl's voice. "I skidded on the wet road is all. And hit a semi. Too bad Clara's seatbelt didn't catch. Now, forget all that bad talk. Give me a nice, big hug—"

Charlie yanked the pistol from his coat pocket. He had meant to use the pillow to deaden the muzzle blast, so he could get away clean. Instead, he cast it angrily aside. Anger also clouded his eyes and kept him from lining up his sights. He jerked the trigger six times, and all six shots went astray.

Lauren, meanwhile, sat coolly dragging on her cigarette. By the way Charlie's pistol wobbled, she knew she had nothing to fear. When her husband's gun clicked empty, she taunted, "Missed as usual, didn't you, dear?"

Watson's face went suddenly pale, and he moaned in utter futility. He began shaking uncontrollably as his last shred of manhood slipped away. When a flood of tears blinded him, he let the pistol clatter to the floor.

"Poor, poor Charlie," cooed Lauren, as she rose to snare him in her embrace. She ran her fingers through his sweat-sodden hair and stroked his streaming cheeks. Then, she wrapped herself around him like a snake until she felt his pulse deaden.

When security finally burst into the room, they found Charlie Watson lying comatose on the bed. Lauren was bent prayerfully over him, weeping like she hadn't just inherited nine hundred grand.

"My husband's had a major breakdown," she sobbed. "Help him. Please! Please, please help dear Charlie."

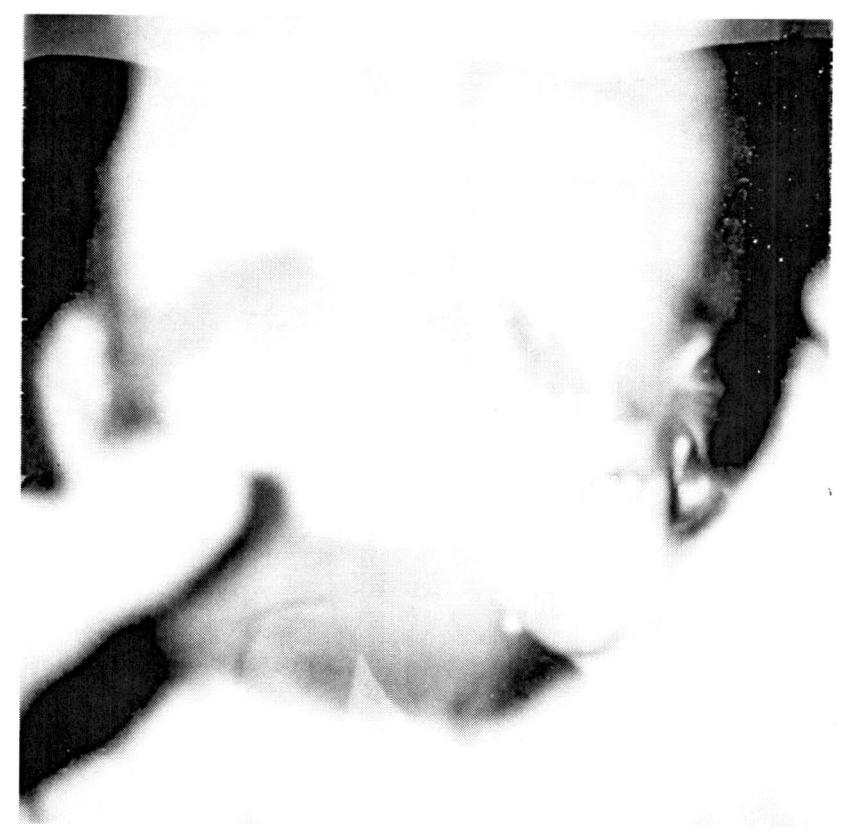

THE RETURN OF LAUREN WATSON

"Dang! Why can't Lauren park her stinkin' sports car farther up the driveway?" grumbled Ben Fairweather as he carefully squeezed his Chevy behind the shiny, gold T-Bird parked at his mother's house. "And after inheriting nine hundred grand, why would she come back here?"

Still muttering under his breath, Ben crawled from his sedan and slammed the door behind him. Dressed neatly in golf slacks and a Ragg Wool sweater, he sloshed across the soggy front lawn toward a modest two-story dwelling. That morning his foursome had been rained out to sour his usually happy mood. That and rumors of his sister's drunken antics that had blown like a sewer-tainted breeze through Blackburn Country Club.

Ben had worked hard to rise from his humble beginnings. He had paid his own way through college by slaving long hours in a meat processing plant butchering hogs that still filled his nightmares with their squeals. Then, he had returned to the same workplace as a management trainee. Now, fifteen years later, he was the director of finances and in line to be appointed CEO. The last thing he needed was for Lauren's bad behavior to cut him off from the good graces of his social peers.

Ben spryly bounded up the steep flight of steps leading to the kitchen. He yanked open the door and found his mother hunched over the sink absently washing her breakfast dishes. She turned at the noise of his entry, and a relieved smile passed across her wizened face. "Son, am I glad you're here," she murmured. "I-I-I was so afraid for you."

"Afraid for me?" echoed Ben.

"I thought Lauren k-k-killed you. With a knife."

"Oh, Mother! Why would you say that?"

"B-b-because she hates you and m-m-me."

Mrs. Fairweather's lips suddenly convulsed with fear, and tears poured from her round eyes. Her hands began to tremble so severely that she dropped a cup onto the linoleum floor. When it shattered with a resounding smash, the whimpering, old woman flew into the protection of her son's arms to sob out her obvious distress.

Ben comforted his mom the best he could. Then, he sat her at the kitchen table, while he swept up the sharp ceramic pieces of the broken cup.

"How could Lauren ever hate you?" he asked while emptying the dustpan into the trash. "Didn't you welcome her with open arms when she returned? And you haven't charged her a dime to stay here these past months."

"Because!" blurted Mrs. Fairweather.

"Because why?"

"Because she asked me h-h-how old I was."

"What's wrong with that?"

"When I said '86,' she yelled, 'Then, why don't you die?' "

Ben's mouth flew open in shock and disbelief. Before he could question his mother further, he heard a bedroom door creak open from down the hall. Turning, he saw a willowy redhead stumbling toward him dressed in rumpled pajamas. Her hair was disheveled, and her face was still creased with sleep. She had an actress' cheekbones and nose and would have been beautiful if not for the ruddy discoloration of her skin.

"So it's you, Brother, who's making this damn racket," wheezed Lauren, fishing a half-crushed cigarette from her pocket. After bending to get a light from the stove burner, she snarled, "Don't you ever stay home?"

"And don't you ever do anything but sleep?"

"I'm independently wealthy. I can do as I please."

"Like wrapping yourself around Hubie Whalen like a snake?"

"Who told you that?" Lauren asked with a devil-ish batting of her eyes.

"It was all over the club this morning. How you got toasted and were carrying on in the bar, at the pool, and later in the parking lot."

"Well, you can't expect me to stay here with Mother all the time. You can see how bad she's getting."

"All I know is that she's afraid of *you*!"

"Don't be silly, Ben. I think Mom has Alzheimer's. Paranoia is part of the package."

"That can't be!" blustered Fairweather. "Look at how neatly she still keeps the house."

"Yeah? Look closer," retorted Lauren, pointing to their mother, who had returned to the sink to rewash the clean dishes already stacked in the strainer.

"I think she's just stressed-out over your drinking. If you must act like a teenybopper, can't you at least be more discreet about it?"

"What fun would that be, Brother dear? Then, I wouldn't be able to watch you squirm."

"You're a bitch, Sis. No wonder Charlie had a major breakdown. No husband could stand you!"

"Poor Charlie," cooed Lauren, slipping into a little girl's voice. "He never could keep up. And I suspect you won't either, Bennie. After all, you're ten years older than me. Don't you remember? You were the 'golden boy,' and I was the 'mistake baby.'"

"Don't call me 'Bennie.' You know how I hate that!"

"Yes, Bennie dear."

Ben growled and pounded the dashboard when he saw Lauren's T-Bird even farther down the driveway than on his last visit. To keep his Chevy out of the road, he had to park bumper-to-bumper with her sporty vehicle. "What in the hell's wrong with Sis?" cried Fairweather as he snapped off his engine. "Is her only purpose in life to be aggravating?"

Ben propelled himself from the driver's seat and stalked across the front yard toward the first floor doorway leading into the cellar. *Man, I hate mowing Mom's lawn,* he thought, *but she has no one else to do her yard work since Dad died last year. His funeral was what brought Lauren back to Blackburn. Yeah, and to keep Mom company was the excuse she used to stay here and besmirch the family's good name.*

Suddenly, Ben came to an abrupt halt when he spied his mother aimlessly circling her flower garden. She continued to shuffle along until she saw him gaping at her. Then, she hobbled to embrace Ben with fear glittering in her eyes.

As Ben held his sobbing mother, he finally realized how feeble she had become. Not only was her back hunched from osteoporosis, but the trembling of her extremities signaled an even more serious condition. It was hard to believe that she was the same woman who had gotten up at four o'clock every morning to clean the house and care for her family before upholstering furniture for twelve grueling hours at Viko. She had always been the model for Ben's own work ethic. To see her like this made his throat constrict with emotion when he croaked, "What are you doing out here, Mom? What's wrong?"

"Lauren cooked dinner. And wouldn't give me any. S-s-she pushed me out the door. Told me to throw myself. Down the stairs. . ."

"We'll see about that!" growled Fairweather. "Sit on the steps, while I go give that daughter of yours a piece of my mind."

With anger blazing in his hazel eyes, Ben fairly flew up the stairs to the second floor and burst into the kitchen. The room billowed with greasy, black smoke that rose from a smoldering pan of fried food still on the stove. Ben choked as the overpowering stench entered his throat and fairly stopped him in his tracks. Fighting his way across the kitchen, he turned off the burner under the pan and then flung open a window to let out the horrid odor.

As Fairweather fought for breath, he became aware of his sister perched on the sofa in the adjacent living room. Her uncombed hair was matted from sweat, and she still wore the same rumpled pajamas he had seen her in a week ago. She was hacking at a huge rare steak that completely dwarfed the plate she cradled in her lap. When he stepped toward her, he could tell she was wasted by the way her eyelids fluttered and how the silverware shook in her hands.

"Well, look who's zere," Lauren slurred as she absently sliced at the bloody meat. "If it ain't Ben Dover."

"Before you call me names, you should take a glance in the mirror. You look like something the cat coughed up. Why don't you check yourself into rehab and clean up your act?"

"And why don't you go to hell?"

"To join you? I don't think so! I oughta come over there and teach you some manners!"

"Come on, then," invited Lauren with a harsh laugh that resounded with more menace than should have come from such a small woman. "Bring it on!"

Stunned by his sister's belligerence, Ben watched aghast as hatred twisted Lauren's face into that of a vicious beast. Tossing aside her knife and fork, she snatched up her steak and took a ferocious bite out of it. She continued to tear at it with her teeth until her chin streamed with juice and gore.

In total disgust, Ben backed from the kitchen and clambered down the steps. Rejoining Mrs. Fairweather, he said, "I'm going to mow the lawn, Mom. Why don't you stay here and watch?"

"W-w-what about L-L-Lauren?"

"She's totally whacked! We'll deal with her later."

Ben unlocked the basement door. Descending into the gloom, he accidentally set off a line of mouse traps that Mrs. Fairweather had stretched across the floor. "Why can't Mom use Decon like everybody else?" he barked, dancing away from the clacking springs. "How she can be afraid of a little rodent is beyond me!"

Too impatient to turn on the light, Ben fumbled in the murk until he tripped unexpectedly over a kitchen chair. "Who in the hell left that here?" he yelped.

"Dang drunken Lauren, no doubt! Probably comes down to guzzle stashed booze."

Finally, Ben grabbed the push mower in his long arms and wrestled it up the steps. Then, he slammed the Toro onto the lawn, filled it with gas, and started it with one vicious pull. Still angry with his sister, he ran around the perimeter of the front yard clipping the grass at a furious pace. He only slowed when he came to an uneven piece of ground near the porch. Carefully, he mowed through the sharp dip like he'd done countless times before. He had just started up the other side when he heard a tremendous snap.

The Toro's engine came to an abrupt halt as the grating of metal resounded in Ben's ears. "Crap!" he growled. "The stinkin' mower blade bent."

"Are you all right?" cried Mrs. Fairweather, rising from the steps in alarm. "Did it cut you?"

"No! No! I only have to replace the blade. I think Dad kept a spare under his workbench."

Brushing past his mom, Ben charged down the cellar steps and flicked on the overhead light switch. He was greeted by a tremendous flash as the light bulb exploded above him, showering him with shards of glass. In fear and disbelief, Fairweather boiled out of the basement and sprinted for his car. Halfway across the yard, his mother's shouts registered in his brain, and he skidded to a stop to sheepishly return to her side.

"I-I-I better go check on Lauren," said Ben, obviously spooked. "That was some surge of electric! I hope she wasn't hurt."

"I better come, too."

"Okay, but stay behind me."

Cautiously, the Fairweathers crept up the steps and creaked open the kitchen door. The house was ominously silent, and it took Ben a moment to work up his courage before stepping inside. The smoke had dissipated, so he had no problem seeing his sister passed out on the couch. Her face bore a glazed look as she snored peacefully into her half-eaten plate of steak.

"It's all right now, Mom," said Ben with a grateful sigh. "You can come in."

"O-o-only if you'll stay with me."

"There's nothing to be afraid of. Lauren's out cold."

"But she'll wake up. And lock me in the cellar again."

"Again?"

"Like last night."

"Oh, Mom, Lauren wouldn't do that. You must have had a nightmare."

"Please stay with me," begged Mrs. Fairweather, clutching her son's arm. "Or take me home with you."

"I can't, Mom. I'm hosting a dinner party for all the company bigwigs. It'll surely get me promoted to CEO. You know how much that will mean for my career."

"Can't I come?"

"No, I have too much to do. Look at how out of it Lauren is. She couldn't hurt anyone. You'll be fine here. And I'll check on you first thing tomorrow morning."

"Promise?"

"Promise."

When Ben drove up to his mother's house at eight a.m., he found Lauren's T-Bird completely blocking the driveway. Snarling in frustration, he shot on past and screeched into the firehouse lot farther down the block.

"So Sis was out already," he grumbled. "I hope she didn't buy more booze."

Troubled by this reflection, Fairweather scrambled from his Chevy and sprinted down the road. His heart pounded as he dashed by his sister's car and on across the half-cut lawn. He was about to ascend the stairs when he remembered the mess in the basement made by the exploding light bulb. "I'd better sweep up that glass," he grunted, "before tackling any new problems."

Ben fished a key from his pocket and snapped open the padlock that fastened the cellar door. As he ducked to enter the basement, he was blinded by sunlight streaming in the window over the workbench. Disoriented by the glare, he stumbled down the steps. At that moment, the sun went behind a cloud to reveal an image that brought a gasp from the bottom of Ben's throat. There, in the center of the floor, sat his mother. She was tied stiffly upright in the kitchen chair he had tripped over the day before. Drool spilled down her stubbly chin. Her eyes stared vacantly at nothing.

Fairweather gasped a second time when he saw why his mother was so fearful of rodents. Two huge sewer rats were gnawing on her bare feet, while another was eating her ear. "Oh, my God!" he shrieked, streaking across the concrete floor to chase off the feasting vermin. "Get away! Get!"

In a panic Ben grabbed his mom's wrist and squeezed it until he felt the rhythm of a faint pulse. Even then, he thought she was dead until he noticed the involuntary twitching of her left arm.

"Lord, forgive me," croaked Ben, "for putting my ambitions before my dear mother. I g-g-gotta g-g-get her to the hospital!"

Fairweather leaped up and shot over to the work-bench. As he rifled feverishly through the drawers, he failed to see his sister steal into the basement like a slipper-footed wraith.

"Is this what you're looking for?" snickered Lauren, brandishing a long knife.

"Don't just stand there!" yelled Ben. "Cut Mom loose!"

"I don't think so, Bennie."

"You don't think so?"

"She'll just fall on the floor. Not that she'd feel how much it'd hurt."

"So you have been abusing Mother! Why?"

"She was mean to me," whined Lauren, assuming the voice of a teenage girl. "She kept taking my cigarettes. And birth control pills. I couldn't date the cool boys, then. Or go to parties or Red House Lake or anything. But you did whatever you pleased. That sucks!"

"But she was only trying to protect you. From yourself."

"That did a lot of good, didn't it?"

"What did you do to Mother?"

"Told her you were dead, is all. I guess she couldn't take the shock of her Biggie Boy's sudden passing. . ."

"What possessed you to do that?"

"What do you mean by 'possessed?' " roared Lauren, as her voice morphed into that of an enraged masculine entity. "Now, it's your turn to feel my wrath!"

Ben ducked as the workbench exploded behind him. Screwdrivers flew past his head to bury themselves in the ceiling, while hammers and handsaws rose magically to swing and hack at his extremities.

The rise in energy became so intense that the panes blew out of the window. Then, cans of paint imploded to drench the cowering man with a rainbow of insane colors. He leaped to his feet to fly out of the room, only to slip in the greasy semi-gloss. Emitting a hapless wail, he fell heavily and broke both his knees.

When Ben was about as defenseless as his mother, he implored, "Lauren, please. Call out to God. Only He can help you now!"

"Help me?" bellowed the mad, thunderous voice. "Why, He can't even save you!"

To drive home her point, Lauren bent to stab her brother savagely in the chest. "Oops!" she mocked. "Where's the breastplate of righteousness?" Kicking him in the head, she howled, "So much for the helmet of salvation!" She continued to pummel and stab at Ben until he felt no more. Then, she calmly dragged his body toward the band saw that had lifted off the workbench and alighted on the floor next to the paneled wall.

Lauren cut her brother into easily hefted hunks. Prying loose a piece of paneling, she stashed the mutilated body behind it. All anger had faded from her face, and she whistled serenely as she hammered the wall board back in place. Mopping up the blood and spilled paint was easy by comparison. She had just removed the rope from her comatose mother when a loud rap came on the cellar door.

"C-c-come in," cried Lauren tremulously. "P-p-please help me."

In the next instant the county deputy burst into the basement followed by several volunteer firemen. "What's going on, miss?" demanded the deputy. "The neighbors called about screaming they heard at your residence."

"It was poor Mom," sobbed Lauren. "She came to do a load of laundry and just freaked out. Her yelling woke me from a sound sleep. By the time I ran downstairs, she was sitting in that chair. Not moving."

"W-w-what set her off?" stammered the blushing fireman, to whom the redhead had run for protection.

"Must have seen a mouse," cooed Lauren, wrapping herself around the firefighter like a snake. "She's frightened to death of them. Don't you see the traps set on the floor?"

"More 'n' a mouse scared this woman," croaked one of the volunteers. "Look at those rat bites!"

For the first time Lauren pretended to notice her mother's gnawed feet. Then, she broke into hysterical tears.

"Now, calm down, miss," urged the deputy. "We have an ambulance parked in the road outside. We'll get your mom right to the hospital. Would you like to come along?"

"No, I'm too weak," moaned Lauren, lapsing into a swoon.

"Don't let her fall!" shouted a burly fireman.

"Don't worry!" screeched the guy who held her. "She's safe with me."

"Get her upstairs!" ordered another volunteer. "I'll grab her legs!"

The firemen carried Lauren Watson up to the living room and placed her gently on the couch. She mumbled a weak "Thank you" as the allured men fell all over themselves trying to make her more comfortable. With crooked grins wreathed on their faces, they fetched for her a blanket, a pillow, and a rum and Coke to settle her nerves. Afterward, she fluttered her hand in answer to their "Goodbyes" and told them to drop by "anytime."

When all was silent again, the redhead rose to fetch a cigarette from her purse. She plopped back on the sofa and lit it with a Zippo lighter she had filched from the cutest fireman's pocket. Then, a satisfied smile spread across her vermillion lips. As she blew smoke rings toward the ceiling, she heard no dripping blood or telltale heart. Instead, she visualized spiders— spiders weaving a winding sheet within the cellar wall.

THE GREAT STAG

The lone hunter slid noiselessly from a thicket of scrub beech and entered a path that wound up a steep mountain choked with brush and trees. The man was clad in a raveled blanket coat and a pair of stained wool pants. A knit cap was crammed over an unruly mop of bootblack hair. A smile played across his weather-cracked lips as he admired the fresh snowfall that made the day perfect for tracking and hunting. After adjusting the scoped rifle cradled in his left arm, he again set his gum boots in motion.

The half-breed worked methodically up the mountain. Often, he stopped to scan the woods around him for the elusive deer he stalked. Each time he paused, he leaned against a trailside tree to conceal his outline. Soon, he began to encounter fresh hoof prints that spilled from the mountainside across his path. That made him even more alert and slowed his pace to a veritable crawl.

The hunter inched along until spotting a distinctive set of boot prints that entered the trail from a bisecting road. Glancing warily from left to right, he felt sweat pop out on his forehead. Before he could bolt for the nearest brush, a warden clad in dark green camo stepped from behind a broad oak to block his escape.

"Where ya goin', Blackie Grimes?" demanded the officer, his hand straying toward the pistol housed on his hip.

"Uh. . .Feeggered I'd follow these deer, Luke," muttered the half-breed, pointing toward a set of pronounced tracks veering up the slope.

"Yeah, right! Where's yer orange clothin'? After I give ya a warnin' an' a fine, ya know durn well that it's illegal to hunt without it."

"Right here, meester," grunted Grimes, turning to reveal a patch of faded blaze cloth stitched crudely to the back of his coat. "I'm wearin' two hundred feefty square eenches of orange. . .like the rule books says. You can measure eff you want."

"That don't cut it! You know as well as me that the orange must be visible from all di-rections. Looks like I get ta run ya in."

"But I's way legal," protested Blackie. "Lookee here."

The half-breed bowed toward Warden Luke. Atop his knit cap was pinned a scrap of reddish yellow yarn that technically fulfilled the limits of the law.

After grumbling to himself, the officer said, "The only difference 'tween you an' a coyote is that you smell worse. But you'll screw up. An' I know you already done potted two deer."

"Even coyotes must eat!" snapped Blackie, forgetting the *five* bucks and the doe he had already shot. Fire blazed in his sullen eyes at the insult. He glared at the tall warden and tightened his grip on his gunstock.

"Yeah, but at least them predators know who's the big dog," growled the lawman, drawing himself up to his full height. "What are ya doin' in these here woods anyhow if'n ya already shot them two deer?"

"Why, I has ze bonus tag," replied the half-breed, again turning to show Luke the extra license holder pinned on his back.

"Which en-titles ya to one extra doe. I'll be watchin' ya, Grimes. You best believe it!"

"Then, you best be able to drive ze truck to the top of that mountain," chuckled Grimes, motioning toward Luke's pickup that was partially concealed by a patch of beech farther down the bisecting road. "That's where I do ze best hunting."

"Ya don't think I can hike up there?" snarled the lanky officer. "Why, I can still walk the legs off a little runt like you any day o' the week, includin' Sunday. See ya at the top. You bet!"

"See you in ze fires of hell!" yipped Blackie, giving the warden a mock salute and a thumb to the nose.

Before the lawman could bark back, Grimes leaped into the nearest thicket and bolted straight up a severe incline that most bears couldn't have climbed. Using saplings and branches for handholds, he struggled upward until he reached the next bench. There, he collapsed in the snow, listening to Luke's faint, windblown curses below.

When the half-breed's breathing returned to normal, he staggered to his feet and found another faint trail that wound around the mountain. Again, he assumed a hunter's stealth and crept along searching the woods with his piercing, pitch-colored eyes. He continued on until he reached the next trail that led steeply upward to the summit. There were deer tracks everywhere, and he licked his cracked lips knowing that he soon would be among the fat doe that swarmed on the ridge top.

Blackie's heart thudded with excitement when he spied a rusted oil tank capsized in the snow ahead. Just behind the overturned tank sat an abandoned powerhouse that marked the beginning of the best hunting territory. The building was made of tin, and its doors yawned open to reveal a long-silent engine that once powered ten creaking rod lines and oil jacks. Now, the powerhouse provided winter refuge for skunks and other small critters. The half-breed grinned as he watched a startled squirrel dart inside. Then, he stomped toward the beech thicket that crowned the peak beyond.

Keeping to the trail, Grimes slunk through a sea of rattling, orange leaves. He moved a step at a time, keeping his eyes trained on the path ahead. He hadn't gone more than a quarter mile when he saw a doe's nose poke from the brush only fifty yards distant. To avoid detection, the hunter slipped into the prone position. He stared through his scope and snicked his rifle off safe.

The lead doe crept stiffly from the beech, sniffing the air for enemies. Cautiously, she peered in all directions before moving to the middle of the trail. Behind her were two yearlings that followed in rote, trusting obedience. The herd barely stepped into the open when the roar of Blackie's .30-40 Krag rent the silence with deadly thunder.

The doe's head exploded in a cloud of hair and gore, and she crashed unmoving to the ground. With stunned bleats, her young ones milled about, staring stupidly into the brush ahead with wild, panicked eyes. As they sidled side-by-side toward their downed mother, a second shot rang out. It was the last sound either of them heard. The bullet tore through the neck of the first yearling and then entered the second just above the front shoulder. Both small doe collapsed in a spray of blood to kick weakly and gurgle one last astonished cry.

Blackie was up and racing toward the deer the instant they fell from the crosshairs of his scope. "Show me a coyote that could do that," cackled the half-breed, still fuming over the warden's insult. "I kill with ze efficiency no beast can match!"

Grimes whipped out a long, wicked-looking skinning knife. He slit each deer's throat in turn to make sure all were good and dead. "Now, I got meat 'til strawberries make ze venison sweet again," he whispered, glancing warily down the trail toward the powerhouse. "Must hide these. Queek! Luke must not see."

The half-breed dragged the mother doe over to a great gray beech blown down by a recent squall. He dug furiously in the snow beneath the trunk and then crammed the deer's carcass in the space he had created. Similarly, he concealed the body of one of the yearlings beneath a neighboring windfall. When he returned to the road to fetch the second small doe, a flight of chickadees sailed from the brush and began circling Blackie's head. The birds beat their wings furiously, calling with angry "deedeedees." They closed within inches of the man's face, slapping at him with their feathers. Their attack was so fierce and persistent that Grimes dropped his gun into the snow to cover his head with both arms. Again and again the chickadees dove at him until finally he lashed out with a big, mittened paw and knocked one of his antagonists from mid-flight.

"What ze hell is wrong with you?" howled the half-breed, stomping the chickadee beneath his gum boots. "Since when such happy birds go crazy?"

The other birds continued to dive at Grimes, who danced and slapped like a honey bear beset by bees. They did not quit their assault until one-by-one they were batted from the sky and tramped into bloody pulps.

Fuming and covered with sweat, Blackie hid the second yearling with her sister. Still distracted, he broke off a branch and brushed away his tracks that led to his deer caches. After sweeping out signs of the does' demise from the snowy road, he stooped to pick up his rifle where the chickadees had attacked him. Cursing in both English and Iroquois, he knocked the snow from the barrel. Next, he cleaned the lens of his scope with a soiled, blue handkerchief that he yanked roughly from his pants pocket. When the .30-40 Krag was safe to fire again, he grunted, "Too early to quit ze hunt. Still have bonus tag. Ha! Ha!"

Blackie cast several furtive glances down the trail behind him. Afterward, he prowled along the ridge looking for more venison on the hoof. His eyes had a murderous cast as he slipped noiselessly through the powdery snow. He skulked along, stopping often to survey the winter-quiet woods. Finally, he paused by a patch of blood-red brambles to blow his nose. As he fished for the oft-used handkerchief, a scolding male grouse erupted from the thicket inches from where Grimes stood. With a surprised gasp, the half-breed leaped back, lost his footing, and toppled to the frozen ground, cracking his skull on a rock. A darkness descended upon him as the rush of wings dissipated down a black slope.

After what seemed like a very long time, Grimes' eyes fluttered open. His vision blurred at each attempt to raise his head, and he was forced to sink groaning back into the snow. It took him six tries before he could sit up. When he finally fought to his feet a half-hour later, he shook his fist in the direction the grouse had flown. "Doddamn you!" he growled. "I come back. You wait! With my shotgun I git you. Warden not always on patrol."

Grimes knocked the snow from his rifle a second time and lurched woozily forward. He hadn't taken more than a step or two when a pileated woodpecker gave a loud, warning cry. The alarm was immediately taken up by a red squirrel and then by blue jays as the half-breed slogged up the ridge. With so many creatures announcing his presence, Grimes stomped angrily through the snow. Finally, he broke into a coyote's lope to lose the pesky sentinels. He trotted and then sprinted with the sharp, reproving voices dogging him. On and on he rumbled, losing track of time and consciousness. The cries seemed to grow louder, the faster he ran.

Grimes raced up the trail until blackness crowded his vision. With a spent grunt, he fell on his face and lay motionless until a swirling wind revived him. When he crawled groggily to all fours, he found himself in a part of the forest he had never hunted. Here, the deadfalls lay buried beneath heavy caskets of snow. Rotten-trunked hemlocks leered at him with knot hole faces, and grave groves of oak creaked in the stiff breeze. A pounding headache magnified this creaking until Blackie clamped his hands over his ears.

A stiff wind probed Grimes' blanket coat like icy corpse fingers. To escape its chilling velocity, he staggered to his feet and followed an oft-used deer trail into a thickly wooded hollow below the ridge top. There, he discovered fresh deer sign everywhere. Tracks crisscrossed the forest floor and led to widespread diggings made by hungry buck and doe. With acorns as thick as marbles beneath the disturbed snow, it was no secret to Blackie why so many deer congregated in such a small yard. He took a second to examine the lofty oaks that towered over him and then returned to his cruel business. Ignoring the pounding in his temples, he looked for a good point of ambush on a prominent crossing.

The half-breed had barely concealed himself behind a massive hemlock when a faint wailing reached his ears. He strained to listen until the cries of "Help! Help!" echoed from the ridge behind him. As the voices drew nearer, they assumed the high-pitched key of lost children. Finally, the carousel of haunted wails swirled directly overhead. With the sky alive with anguish, Blackie felt the gooseflesh rise on his extremities, and he hunkered closer to the trunk that sheltered him.

Doubting his own sanity, Grimes glanced upward and saw the boiling clouds part to reveal a broken flight of geese flailing the dark sky with their wings. Grinning uneasily, he snapped his rifle off safe and muttered, "So it's you who cause ze racket. Must be echo of hollow that makes you sound like leetle kids. I should knock you from ze flight for scaring Blackie so!"

Although thoroughly spooked, Grimes shifted his scrutiny to the deer crossing he hoped would bring him a huge buck. He had seen fresh scrapings on every sapling he had passed since entering this mountain sag. By the length and breadth of these buck rubs, he knew they had been made by more than a spike or four point polishing its antlers. He licked his lips greedily at the thought of such a buck and tried to control the shaking that still made aiming his rifle a chore.

Grimes raised his .30-40 Krag and peered through the scope. Carefully, he looked down the trail to make sure he had a clear shooting lane. No sentinel birds gave him away this time as a foreboding silence gripped the wood. It wasn't long before he discerned the faint crunching of snow just below him to the left. With his pulse pounding in his ears, he raised his rifle again only to find the scope completely fogged. As he dug frantically for his handkerchief, the heavy footsteps of the approaching beast grew louder and louder and LOUDER.

Just as the head of a Great Stag popped over the rise, Blackie yanked his handkerchief free and began swabbing madly at the obscured lens. Not that he needed any magnification to see the massive rack bobbing toward him atop the hugest deer he had encountered in twenty years of hunting. The buck's back was five feet high, and its legs were big around as a draft horse's. Enraged grunts rose from the beast's brawny, white throat. Steam poured from its flared nostrils. Its eyes had a mad cast to them. The antlers appeared even more impressive with each powerful step the buck took. Blackie's mouth flew open in amazement when he counted twenty-five points on the wicked-looking horns.

No matter how hard the half-breed rubbed his scope lens, he could not wipe away the fog. The stag now closed within fifty feet and dropped its head to charge the quivering hunter. With the pounding of hooves throbbing in Blackie's skull, he whipped up his rifle and blindly yanked the trigger. Instead of the roar he expected, there was the sick thud of a firing pin striking a dud cartridge.

Before Grimes could chamber another round, the huge buck rose on its hind legs and lashed out with its left, front hoof. The blow smashed Blackie's nose to jam and shook the rifle from his quivering hands. As the hunter tottered, spewing blood, a swirling wind filled the hollow with a strange, priest-like chant. "I am Divine," it droned. "I am Divine."

The buck punched with its other front hoof, knocking out Grimes' teeth. As more gore squirted from his pulverized face, the half-breed suddenly remembered the three doe he had slaughtered on the ridge. With a whimper, he dropped to his knees and raised his hands in a prayerful, pleading pose.

The Great Stag bent down and thrust its saber-like antlers through Blackie's chest. The next instant Grimes was lifted flailing into the air. He gurgled as blood filled his lungs. Flung skyward like a broken scarecrow, he emitted a hollow, helpless shriek. He hit the ground heavily, staring wide-eyed at the snorting, outraged beast towering above him. Then, there was nothing but blackness as a flurry of kicks hammered him into the gory snow.

An hour later, a warden dressed in green camouflage slipped to the lip of the hollow. Luke had been following Blackie's footprints for miles, and he paused to catch his breath and listen to the creaking of the frozen trees.

"Ain't never knowed an Indian ta hunt in a place like this," whispered the warden noting the knothole faces glowering at him from a stand of rotted hemlock. "Grimes must be addled by that fall he took back yonder. . .or outta his stinkin' mind!"

To calm his apprehension, the lanky warden concentrated on following the half-breed's boot tracks. They led him down a well-pronounced deer trail into the bowels of a dank oak grove interspersed with witch-haired pines. There, the tracks were more difficult to follow, often disappearing among a multitude of fresh deer diggings.

As Luke glanced about the spooky glen, a grim smile flickered on his face. He grinned again when he remembered the strange way he had found the doe cached by the half-breed just beyond the powerhouse. He still could not believe that in the middle of the day a nocturnal owl had swooped and knocked off his hat, forcing him to stop where a faint spray of deer blood stained the trail. Then, some nuthatches squawked and carried on so in the underbrush that the officer went there to investigate. Just a single drop of gore near a half-swept boot track led to his discovery of the two yearlings. With that, the warden had enough evidence to lift Blackie's hunting license and keep him out of the woods for a very long time.

"Serves the bugger right!" muttered Luke with a renewed burst of energy. "I'm gonna love bustin' Grimes once I catches up with him."

The lawman sneaked a little faster, taking long, silent strides through the snow. It had become eerily quiet, and he swore he heard the excited "deedeedees" of a ghostly flock of chickadees as he slipped along. Although he peered intently into the oak branches above him, he caught not one glimpse of the black-capped birds.

Finally, the warden rounded a bend and found where Grimes' boot tracks came to an abrupt halt. At the exact moment he spotted the horribly mauled body of the half-breed, a blast of icy wind stabbed through his coat. With chattering teeth, Luke bent to examine what was left of the poacher he had hunted for so long. Blackie's entire face was bashed in. His front teeth were missing. His nose was mashed gristle. One eye socket was vacant. The other housed an inky pupil bulged in unspeakable agony.

Luke turned and vomited into the snow. Wiping his mouth on his mitten, he continued his examination. It was then that he saw the jagged wound ripped by huge antlers the length of Blackie's chest.

"So a buck got 'im," muttered Luke. "An' here I thought some ticked off landowner beat 'im to a pulp. The little bugger musta poured a whole bottle of doe scent on himself to get a buck so riled. Yet, I don't smell nothin'."

The officer ran his hands over Grimes' rent ribs and on down his legs. Every major bone had been shattered by what Luke concluded were wicked hoof blows. When the grunts of a great buck resounded up the gully below him, he snatched a stout rope from his jacket pocket and tied a loop in one end. Feverishly, he worked the loop over the corpse's head, around its shoulders, and up under its armpits. Pulling the slipknot tight, he began dragging what was left of Blackie Grimes from the haunted hollow.

"No need ta get a party of fellas with a stretcher," said Luke, glancing nervously about. "Ain't e-nough left of Grimes fer that. Couldn't git no durned volunteers to come *here*, anyhow. . ."

Luke pulled for all he was worth as the wind washed away his last words. Its swirling intensified until it assumed the howling pitch of a living thing. "I am Divine" the wind shrieked just as Luke saw a Great Stag step from behind a hundred-year-old oak to shake a huge set of horns stained with bright gore.

The warden didn't remember much after that. He lowered his head and charged uphill, his legs pumping like pistons. The exact moment the rope broke, he didn't know. Nor did he care what became of the corpse of Blackie Grimes. He had felt the breath of that Stag on the back of his neck and the breeze from those slashing antlers. All he knew is that he made it to the ridge top.

Yes, and now Luke could just see the old powerhouse ahead through a rattling screen of orange beech. He still didn't dare turn around. All he could do was run. Run for the road at the foot of this very scary mountain. The mountain that killed those who violated its laws and creatures.

BLOOD-HUNGRY BEASTS

"This doesn't look a bit familiar," muttered Professor Blaine Richardson, glancing up the dirt trail through a maze of chest-high ferns and second growth ash and cherry. "That'll teach me to get such a late start. Guzzling all that vodka with Dr. Williams fogged my brain. I should have crossed a long meadow by now. . ."

Fighting back the dry heaves, Blaine collapsed on a log to reflect on his morning misadventures. Although he knew it was a six mile hike to the native brook trout stream he planned to fish that day, he never crawled out of the sack until ten-thirty. His queasy stomach had made breakfast out of the question, other than the Pepsi he had choked down. After gathering up his fly rod, waders, and fishing vest, he had staggered out to his Jeep Cherokee and ground on the starter for two minutes before the engine finally sputtered into life. It wasn't until halfway to the stream that he had remembered the fly box sitting on his workbench. That caused even more delay as he did a dangerous u-turn on Route 6 and shot back to his off-campus apartment. By the time his Jeep finally bounced down the old railroad grade to the trailhead leading to Doe Run, his stomach was a total wreck. Even worse, the sun had completed half its day's journey toward the East Branch Dam to the west.

As Richardson crawled groggily to his feet, he remembered the old ridge runner who first told him about the wonderful brookie fishing in Doe Run. Blaine had met the gabby fellow at Skeeter's Inn after a baseball game. Although the codger was well in his cups, he had warned over and over to always veer right when traveling this trail. "Hell of a place ta git lost," he had slurred by way of conclusion. "Hell of a place."

"Oh, man," groaned Blaine. "I went left at the first fork I came to. That was more than an hour ago. It's too late to backtrack now, or I'll never get to wet a line before dark. This path must hit the stream somewhere, and I just have to try those new nymph patterns I've been working on for so long. Tying them was the only thing that kept my sanity while teaching jerk-off pilot freshmen all summer. I guess my teaching days are all but over now. At least I still have the woods for a refuge!"

With a determined scowl, the fisherman again stumbled up the trail. As he worked his way through the dense forest, he saw no other boot prints in the soft mud beneath his feet. That didn't mean that the path wasn't well-traveled, though, as a multitude of deer tracks kept the grass from intruding onto the lane. There were also plenty of coon prints tipped with impressive claws. Several times what looked like loping dog tracks chased prominently along.

"Must be damn coyotes," Blaine muttered nervously, remembering the holstered pistol he had left sitting on the kitchen counter by his backdoor. "Whoever let those varmints loose should be shot! Timber companies most likely were the culprits. They're always whining about the deer ruining the forest. Never did see a doe that could chomp as many trees as a chainsaw. But coyotes? They can eat their weight in fawns and snow-fatigued bucks."

Another hour's hike brought Blaine to the edge of a steep slope leading to a glistening stream below. The downhill path was littered with loose stones that made footing treacherous. The professor held onto his camouflage fishing cap as he skidded most of the way to the bottom. The struggle to keep his balance tested an athletic ability proven on countless ball diamonds and football fields. The murmuring of the brook urged him on until he slid to a halt near its fern-choked bank.

With a shiver, Richardson wiped clammy sweat from his forehead. "Man, it's getting chilly," he said, "and judging by the sun, it can't be more than three o'clock. Sure wish I'd worn something heavier than this canvas shirt. It wouldn't have hurt to bring along a sandwich, either. All that walking cured my hangover and left me hungrier than hell!"

The fisherman snapped together his fly rod and threaded the line through the guides. His fingers trembled with anticipation as he tied a hare's ear nymph onto his leader and crept to the edge of the gurgling, freestone stream. Staying low to avoid detection, he flicked the fly with a practiced cast into the current by an undercut bank. The nymph barely hit the water when a dark streak shot out and grabbed it — hard. Blaine set the hook and felt his line tug with a heavy fish. The brookie dove deep and tried to entangle the leader in some roots beneath the bank. Somehow, the angler steered the fish away from the snag and guided it downstream. The brookie splashed and pulled and splashed some more before Richardson was able to yank it out of the water.

"What a fine native!" gasped Blaine, admiring the ten inch beauty he had landed. "Look how black he is. That's from living under that bank. If he stayed more in the riffles, he'd be silver. And look at those orange fins and blood red spots on his side. It's almost a shame to kill such a fish."

Richardson put his thumb in the brookie's mouth and snapped its neck. Then, he inserted the thin blade of his filet knife into the fish's bung hole. He slit its belly up to the gills and removed the innards. Checking the trout's stomach, he found it stuffed with grubs and small insects.

"Yeah, flies will do the trick, all right," chuckled Blaine. "I'd better stash this fish in my vest and get moving."

The fisherman crept slowly up the stream bank until he came to a place where a log had fallen into the water, forming a deep pool. Richardson had learned from his angler dad that it was best to fish upstream because feeding trout always faced in that direction.

Staying below them lessened the chances of spooking the fish. All wild trout were extra skittish with bears and coons after them, too.

"Every creature has its natural enemies," said Richardson with a bitter laugh. "Even college profs."

Blaine flicked his fly to the exact spot the current gushed under the log. In an instant he was fast to another brookie, and the fight was on. This fish stayed deep and made slashing runs up and down the pool. It was too large to jerk from the water and too fast to stop.

"Can't horse this monster!" jabbered the angler, frantically feeding out line. "My 4X leader won't stand the strain!"

Expertly, Blaine worked the fish until it tilted exhausted on its side. He slid the brookie onto a sand beach and pounced on it just as the hook pulled free. Before the fish could flop back into the water, Richardson scooped the fifteen inch native into his huge paws.

"Wow!" whooped Blaine. "I've never seen a native this size. Look at that hooked jaw. Maybe I should take the wrong trail more often!"

Flushed with excitement, Richardson cleaned his catch and charged upstream hoping for more trophy-sized brookies. His early success made his casts sloppy and his approach less stealthy. Now, he began spooking and losing more fish than he landed. He also fell frequently into the creek and was drenched by the time he hauled in his eighth legal trout miles from where he had entered this valley.

Blaine flopped wearily to his knees on a mossy stretch of stream bank. He was weak from exertion and lack of food. He felt dizzy and a little scared when he saw how the shadows had lengthened with early evening.

After peeling off his heavy vest, Richardson reached inside the back pouch and produced a bag overflowing with trout. He laid his catch on the ground and measured each fish with a rusty ruler. With an awed gasp, he counted one fifteen incher, three twelve inchers, three ten inchers, and a nine incher.

"This is the best limit of brookies I've ever caught," wheezed Blaine. "Yeah, and I guess I'm equally adept at catching hell. . ."

One-by-one Richardson gave his fish a thorough cleaning. He inserted his thumb inside each trout's belly and scraped away all traces of the black membrane coating the spine. Then, he ripped out the remaining red gill fragments that could cut a man's fingers to ribbons if he wasn't careful. Afterward, he rinsed his fish in the cold waters of the stream to wash away the slime coating their skin. With a wide grin, he placed the fifteen incher in the bottom of a fresh plastic bag and then slid the smaller brookies on top of it.

"That should keep these boys from spoiling," said Blaine. "They're too good eating to waste. The way my stomach's rumbling, maybe I should build a fire and roast them on the coals. I'm going to have to if I can't find my way out of here."

Weighed down by his heavy catch, Richardson tramped off downstream. His legs felt like rubber, and his eyes had a glazed look about them. Thigh-high ferns made the going rough whenever he strayed far from the brook. The stream banks proved equally treacherous. Often, he skidded on slippery rocks and twice fell on his face.

After a grueling hour's death march, he finally reached the trail leading to the ridge top. Blaine fell four more times on the loose gravel as he struggled up the steep path. His waders had rubbed his feet raw, too. His gait displayed a pronounced limp by the time he struggled to the summit.

The sun was now close to dropping below the horizon, and Blaine still had a long way to walk to reach his Jeep. With renewed urgency, he stumbled up the ridge through the darkening woods. He trudged bravely along, letting his feet find the way. With the evening gloom dogging him, he continued on until he reached the rim of another valley completely unknown to him.

Richardson jerked to a halt and stared down a long incline choked with hemlock. "What the hell?" he mumbled. "Must have made another bleeping wrong turn. But where?"

With a weary groan, Blaine did an about-face and limped back the way he had come. Forcing himself to stay alert, he searched in vain for the trail leading to his vehicle. Instead, he ended up where he had begun — on the slope above the stream he had fished all afternoon.

Blaine collapsed and buried his head in his hands. "Stayed too long. Drank too much," he groaned through clenched fingers. "Drank way too bleeping much. . ."

Richardson continued to grumble and curse until the call of a great owl chided him from a shadowy stand of cherry. This hooting filled Blaine with unreasonable anger. Scrambling to his feet, he clambered back down the slope and ran headlong into the thick ferns. With panic jumbling his brain, he raced in circles, not knowing or caring where he ran. Often, he fell or smacked into trees until exhaustion knocked his churning legs out from under him.

When the craziness faded from his eyes, Blaine sat up and mumbled, "What to do? What to do? Why, I must be somewhere in Doe Run. Maybe if I go upstream, I'll find the trail I'm familiar with. That will get me back, sure as hell. But how far will I have to walk to get there? Maybe I'd better. . .go downstream. To the East Branch Dam. I'm bound to find someone there. To help me."

A hopeful smile flickered across Blaine's lips. Steadying himself against a scabby-barked cherry trunk, he rose on wobbly legs and staggered off down the creek bank. With darkness closing fast, he used the gurgling voice of the brook to guide him.

Richardson limped tentatively along until a flushing grouse erupted from the ferns. He sprang back in surprise and then dove on his knees to search madly for a baseball-sized rock. Clutching the missile in his hand, he jumped up just as a second grouse took wing. With a low growl, Blaine flung the stone to knock the grouse from mid-flight. Baring his teeth, he leaped on the flopping bird and wrung its neck. "Still got my pitching arm," he babbled. "And now I got meat, too. Time to build a fire. Time to eat. You bet!"

In the last glimmer of twilight, Richardson gathered a pile of dry twigs. Urgently, he rifled through the pockets of his fishing vest until he found the matches he had stashed there. The box was soggy from his tumbles into the creek. The first match would not strike on the slick side of it. With trembling fingers, Blaine ruined others on a dew-soaked rock. In desperation, he struck his last match on the zipper of his pants. The head crumbled before igniting, leaving Blaine to curse his ill luck. Although he could not cook the grouse, he stuffed it in his vest pouch with the limit of trout.

Gripped again by panic, the fisherman dashed along the creek bank, crashing through patches of ferns and beech brush. His path was now guided by an eerie full moon that rose suddenly over the black hills. The temperature had dropped sharply with the falling of night, and Blaine exhaled clouds of frosty breath as he sprinted downstream.

Finally, Richardson charged from the woods onto a brushy plain. There, he encountered a broad dirt road that circled the glittering waters of the East Branch Dam. With a joyful shout, Blaine danced in the moonlight and raised his arms triumphantly like a victorious marathon runner. "I'm saved! I'm saved!" he blared. "I'll bet this track leads to the new campground the state built on the reservoir last spring."

The fisherman continued to frolic until the foul odor of grouse guts wafted from his vest to choke out his celebration. Turning, he started west up the road only to learn that his panicked exit from Doe Run had turned his feet into a mass of oozing blisters. A searing pain accompanied each step and sent his stomach into fresh convulsions. When his agony became unbearable, Blaine unsheathed his knife and hacked down an ash sapling that grew next to the road. Dropping to one knee, he trimmed off the branches and cut the stout stick to a five-foot length. As he sharpened one end, he said, "This will make a dandy staff. Nothing's going to stop me now."

Richardson rose and started once more up the dirt track. The road led across a meadow and into another dense wood. It became steeper there as it wound along a rocky hillside. Although the walking stick alleviated some of the pressure from Blaine's feet, it could not keep his legs from cramping with the added exertion of the uphill climb. The full moon dipped beneath some clouds, making the going even tougher. With an exasperated groan, Blaine sought shelter in a laurel thicket. Exhausted from his trials, he lay down among the bushes and fell instantly asleep.

Somewhere in his dreams, Blaine found himself in a classroom crammed with unruly students. Although they had college-age faces, they pulled the pranks of junior high brats. Spit wads splattered on the blackboard behind him. A flight of paper airplanes barely missed his face. A fart echoed from a back corner. Boogers flicked from fingers found their mark on a shy, black girl's cheek. "What do ya mean I's gonna fail?" growled a surly voice. "You wouldn't last an hour in my hood, teacha!" An imposing freshman dressed in gangsta leather and a do-rag rose from his desk and swaggered threateningly to the front of the class, waving his red-marked test. He grabbed Blaine's arm and twisted it until the professor's free fist lashed out and bashed the punk square in the mug. The bullying, Tysonesque sneer disappeared in a shower of flying teeth to be replaced by a panel of dour-faced deans. The faces closed to within inches of the accused prof and began clucking in self-righteous judgment. "Professors have rights, too. I had to defend myself!" cried Blaine. "I can't believe you're going to sack me for maintaining order in my own classroom — "

A shiver passed through Richardson. He woke with a start. He crawled freezing from the brush and began pacing stiffly on the moonlit road. His thin shirt had done little to protect him from the frosty night, but that only partially accounted for his trembling. Rubbing his arms to restore their circulation, he growled angrily, "Damn bleeping protocol! Damn it to hell! There wasn't time to call security. Didn't they know that?"

By the position of the moon, the professor could tell it was not yet midnight. He lay down again until the frost-laden air returned him to his pacing. "No wonder I stayed too long and drank too much," he grumbled after scrambling from the laurel. "Punks are punks no matter what color they come in. Trustees say we must save our inner city youth. I don't have a problem with giving these kids a chance. . .but not an unfair advantage. Yeah, and just how much will they learn if bad grades or behavior can't fail them? I'm no babysitter. Screw the summer pilot program! And screw the university for sponsoring such a beast! I still can't believe that gangster's strutting around campus instead of behind bars where he belongs. Man, I was the one who was assaulted!"

Richardson lay down a third time. He had just begun to doze off when a haunted howl echoed from the trees near the reservoir. Moments later, it was answered by a closer baying above him on the ridge. Soon, a third howl emitted up the road behind him.

Stealthily, Blaine rose from the bushes and slipped back onto the trail. Using his walking stick to great effect, he worked his way in the direction of the camping area he hoped was not far. The moon popped from the clouds to bathe the woods in an otherworldly glow. Often, the fisherman caught glimpses of the shimmering reservoir just off to his left. He continued to hobble along until he heard the excited yips of a pack of coyotes gathering close to where he had bedded down. With fear surging through his veins, Richardson broke into a painful sprint.

The dirt track climbed steeply upward before leveling off at the next hillside bench. A few yards ahead, laurel flanked the road on both sides, forming an eerie, black tunnel. Blaine didn't want to be trapped there of all places. Afraid his fly rod would get tangled in the bushes, he flung it aside. He darted forward again just as a pack of slathering canines came bounding up the road toward him.

131

Why in the hell are they after me? asked Richardson's brain as he streaked as fast as his blistered feet would allow. *I thought they were afraid of humans. But then freshmen aren't supposed to attack their professor, either. Has this whole bleeping world gone crazy? Can't these coyotes catch my man's scent by now?*

No! screamed his instincts. *Not with that grouse still in your vest. Run, man. Run!*

With the coyotes snarling at his heels, Blaine rushed up the laurel tunnel into total darkness. The excited yips and snapping of sharp teeth made him dash faster than any track opponent he had raced in his prime. Finally, he broke into the open woods where the moon's floodlight glare revealed a ghastly sight. There, just a few yards ahead, he saw that the trail ended at the edge of a precipice.

"So much for finding that campground," croaked Blaine. "I'm on a bleeping fire road!"

Richardson skidded to a halt inches from the brink of a hundred foot drop into the reservoir below. With beads of sweat glinting on his forehead, he gaped into the chasm. The lead coyote, drunk on bloodlust, wasn't as lucky. Off it shot into nothingness, ki-yiing fearfully as it plunged to its death.

Richardson whipped around and thrust his walking stick like a spear just as the second coyote lunged for him. The force of the beast's leap drove the stick deep into its chest, and it fell thrashing to the ground. Moments later, it also flopped over the cliff, leaving four more snarling curs to contend with. Blaine yanked out his filet knife and slashed madly at the next bold beast. A lucky swipe lopped off the end of the coyote's nose, and it turned and fled back into the laurel.

The last three canines attacked in unison. Blaine dodged at the last second, and the curs sprang past him and on over the cliff to join their dispatched kindred. With a victorious whoop, Richardson turned to leave the brink of the precipice only to find his path blocked by the wheezing, wounded coyote. With moonfire gleaming in its eyes, the beast leaped at the professor and planted its fangs in his thigh. Blaine dared not back up. Grabbing his antagonist by the ears, he dove on top of the coyote and wrestled it savagely to the ground.

Back and forth the man and beast rolled, with neither able to gain the advantage. Blaine's limbs streamed with blood as he buffeted the coyote with his hammer-hard hands. The animal slashed with its fangs, oblivious to the heavy blows pummeling its back and flanks.

Finally, in desperation, Blaine latched onto the coyote's throat. The beast kicked and rolled in a mad repeated motion, but the man would not loosen his grip. With all the energy it could muster, the coyote pitched toward the cliff, dragging the professor behind it. Snarling viciously, Richardson throttled the beast until its windpipe popped. As he tried to untangle himself from his suffocating enemy, he felt the rocky soil of the cliff dissolve into rushing air.

Hurtling toward the water below, Blaine thought about the fork he had missed in the trail. There wasn't much for him to return to, anyway. Drinking too much and staying too long was just as much a part of being a man as standing up to coyotes and punks in do-rags. He closed his eyes as he felt the frigid wind numb his senses. The waves heaved up to greet him. Then, there was a black silence devoid of the slathering jaws of deans, trustees, and other blood-hungry beasts.

THE SAME DAMN REBS

California Joe lay hidden in a pine thicket on the edge of a bleak swamp. Clad in the forest green uniform of Berdan's Sharpshooters, only his watery, blue eyes were visible among the shadowy boughs. He was a short man with shoulder-length brown hair, and his face was furrowed from the anxiety of imminent combat. As the crackle of gunfire washed steadily toward him from the right flank, he could also hear the nervous fidgeting of the other members of Company C. His concealed mates were fanned out at five yard intervals to either side of him.

As Joe peered expectantly toward the high ground across the bog, his thoughts returned to other fights he'd weathered while prospecting out West. Sweat shimmered on his brow when he remembered his tense pistol duel with the hombre he blasted in the Gold Dust Saloon. Equally deadly was the time he'd repulsed two bushwhackers on Greenhorn Creek armed only with a shovel. Now, it was his turn to do the bushwhacking as a skirmisher for the Union army's elite rifle regiment.

Suddenly, the woods exploded with the deafening roar of enemy cannons and muskets. It became so instantly loud that the commands of officers could not be heard above the din. At that instant, a horde of howling Rebs added to the tumult until Joe feared that the prophecies of "Revelation" were being visited upon the earth. The blare of a bugle caused him to return fire, and soon the crack of his own rifle was the only noise that mattered.

The Confederate lines of gray and butternut advanced steadily through the jungle-green, summer woods. The Stars and Bars fluttered above the insurgents' heads like a blood-sopped sheet as they stopped every few yards to fire and reload their smoothbores. The air was then filled with so many balls that to Joe they sounded like the hiss of serpents whizzing overhead. Showered by pine branches, he did more ducking than shooting back.

When a lower volley blew up dirt around California, he gave prayerful thanks that he was armed with a Sharps rifle. Lovingly, he patted his breechloader before inserting another linen cartridge. If he'd have had to work a ramrod down a muzzleloader, Joe knew the Rebs would have pinpointed him long before now and smoked him.

The Rebels fixed bayonets and charged to dislodge the thin line of sharpshooters that harried them. They advanced double-quick, yipping like dogs whose tails had been banged in a barn door. Joe and his squad were now firing ten shots a minute and opened up huge gaps in the enemy ranks. By the time the Rebs had reached the swamp, half their number lay littered behind them on the long, bloody slope. One of the last to fall was their wildly-bearded colonel. California drilled him through the forehead as he waved the regimental colors to rally his men.

Driven forward by their remaining officers, the Confederates plunged waist-deep into the muddy bog. In an instant, a deadly swarm of fifty-two caliber bullets ripped through their midst, filling the air with bloody spray. Shrieking their disdain, the Virginians slogged on until only eight rods separated them from the Yankees' blazing Sharps. They got so close that California only had to point his rifle to blow gory holes in the fanatical Rebs' chests. He continued to fire until his barrel was too hot to touch and the last riddled corpse sank into the swamp.

After the sharpshooters' deadly barrage, the groans of the dying were quickly replaced by the whine of mosquitoes. Joe was too fatigued to rise from hiding or even wave off the insects that pestered him. He stared straight ahead until a nearby voice rumbled, "Bully shooting, men. Now, if the gallinippers would quit bitin', we'd be all set."

"Tell that to them fellas we jess slaughtered," muttered Joe, wiping the sweat from his powder-blackened face. "They had as much chance as mastodons trapped in a tar pit, lieutenant."

"Well, we did what we was ordered, Californy. We stopped them Rebs, even if Berdan weren't here to lead us."

Joe glanced sharply toward Ed Wilson after the lieutenant's insinuation. Ed was a solidly built man with dark chin whiskers and a stern face. Like many of the other officers, he had become openly critical of the sharpshooters' commander.

"Then, let's go find the colonel, an' tell him how good we done," blurted California with a wry grin.

"Didn't hear no bugle sound recall," grunted Wilson, "so we best stay put. Us boys would get court-martialed if *we* went berry pickin'."

Hunkering farther into the brush, Joe closed his aching eyes. They had been bothering him more than usual, and he wished he had a pair of smoked glasses to keep out the glare. After he had rested for a short time, he uncorked his canteen and took a swig of stale water. It made him gag, so he poured the rest down his rifle barrel to dissolve the black powder accumulated there. Then, he swabbed out his Sharps to keep it in good working order for the next action.

When the wind died down before sunset, the evening became unbearably hot. Joe wished he was anywhere but this steamy Virginia swamp, and he squirmed uncomfortably in his heavy wool jacket. He unfastened all but the top button and felt instantly better. After that, he must have dozed off because the next thing he remembered was Lieutenant Wilson hissing, "Here they come again, men. At my command, give 'em hell!"

Joe rolled over on his stomach and gazed ahead through the trees. Darkness had now fallen, and the rising moon bathed the woods in an otherworldly glow. Sure enough, down the ridge slipped a wave of Rebels following exactly the same route that the other attackers had used. Alternately moving from shadow to light, they loped along as though totally unconcerned with the whereabouts of the enemy.

When the Confederates closed to within two hundred yards, Wilson bellowed, "Fire!" Flushed by their earlier success, the U.S. Sharpshooters answered with a murderous salvo that raked the woods and filled the muggy air with thick smoke. Moments later, a gasp escaped from the Union ranks when it was learned that not a single Reb had been hit.

"Are you men shootin' blanks?" howled the lieutenant, gaping in disbelief.

"It's the shadows that's to blame," yelped California. "Look! Now, them Rebs is only a hundred yards off. Can't miss 'em this time!"

The skirmishers unleashed another thunderous volley and waited for the smoke to clear. Still, the Confederates had not lost a single man, and even stranger, did not return fire. Instead, they trotted dead-on toward the bewildered Federals as though they were rendezvousing with Stonewall Jackson.

"It's like we's shootin' through 'em!" cried a rifleman to Joe's left.

"Yeah, why ain't they fallin'?" wailed another sharpshooter. "All bunched up like they is, we could jerk the dang trigger an' hit 'em!"

As Company C aired its frustration, Joe rose to the sitting position to get a clearer shot at the enemy. Digging his left elbow into the earthen bank in front of him also afforded the sniper a much steadier rest. After taking a deep breath, he trained his sights on the chest of a distant officer, who was waving the Reb colors to urge his men forward. California then squeezed the trigger until the gun surprised him when it went off.

Joe kept his cheek tight to the stock well after the report of the rifle had echoed off down the line. Yet even after he had displayed perfect shooting mechanics, the bullet had somehow missed its mark. This became immediately evident when Joe spotted his target leading a charge of zombie-like Rebels into the swamp just opposite him.

"Dad gum it!" cussed California. "I couldn'ta missed! Weren't no brush 'tween him an' me. I had a perfect shot!"

It was then that the flag flapped away from the Confederate commander's head, and in the moonlight Joe saw a wildly-bearded face that caused him to leap to his feet. "Fall b-b-back, men," he stammered. "We's f-f-fightin' the same d-d-damn Rebs we k-k-killed this afternoon! No wonder Berdan s-s-stayed behind! Fall back, while we still c-c-can!"

THE EIGHTH WONDER OF THE WORLD

From an overlook built on a rocky hillside, Erik Johnson stared in awe at the Kinzua Viaduct that stretched from ridge top to ridge top 2,053 feet across the valley. The massive structure rose on twenty steel-plated legs from the murky gorge below. In clearer weather he would have seen that the center of the span was over three hundred feet tall. Even obscured by the July rain, to Johnson the viaduct still lived up to its billing as the Eighth Wonder of the World.

Watching the mist swirl about the black bridge, Erik said to his sister who stood shivering beside him, "Hell of a day for Dad's funeral. I guess we better carry out his last request before another downpour drenches us."

"Yes, it seems weird coming here from such a solemn service," sighed Ruby, "especially after all the great times we had at this bridge picnicking with Grandma B."

"I just wish I'd been around in 1900 to see our great grandfather help rebuild the viaduct with steel. I always heard he was a fine Swedish craftsman. He also must have known a bit about having kids if you consider Grandma's ten siblings," chuckled Erik.

"How can you joke at a time like this?" snapped Ruby, tears welling in her blue eyes. "You're the one who's going to spread Dad's ashes over the Kinzua Valley."

"Then, let's get to it before I lose my nerve."

Erik left the overlook and led Ruby up a worn trail to the Kinzua Bridge State Park information area. He walked directly to the photos encased in glass. He knew the images traced the history of the viaduct, and he was drawn to them every time he visited. These pictures were like old friends to him.

He was still amazed that a group of forty industrious men erected the prefabricated ironwork of the original bridge in just ninety-four days. That was in 1882 when all the workers had to aid them were two steam hoists, a gin pole, and a wooden crane. As he studied the crew's faces, Erik saw the same stubborn persistence that was ingrained in his own character.

"Are you going to stand there gawking all day?" whined Ruby, elbowing her brother in the ribs. "Come on. I'm cold."

"I'll bet you wouldn't be cold if we were looking for the gold buried out here," smiled Erik. "You know how many hours Uncle Dick has spent searching for it."

"Yeah. Yeah. I know all about the bank robber who hid his loot by a triangular rock within sight of the bridge. At least all of Dick's snooping allowed him to spot the rust that's been eating away at the support columns for years. I'm glad he told so many people. Without his lobbying, funds never would have been raised to begin the preservation work. Maybe we shouldn't go out there if Uncle Dick says the bridge is unsafe."

"No, it's all right. The state still hasn't closed it to foot traffic."

"I don't know. . .I'll bet if the repair crew guys weren't rained out today, they'd forbid us to walk over the gorge."

Erik turned up his collar as another squall sent a group of tourists scurrying for cover. A little rain couldn't drive him away after all the time he had spent in winter weather with his dad hunting the whitetail deer that teemed near the bridge. Just up the valley, in the middle of a snowstorm, he had shot his first buck near Grant's Rocks. These rocks were named after President Ulysses S. Grant who came to McKean County to hunt with Kinzua Bridge founder, Thomas Kane, and killed a massive stag there. Although Erik's buck was only a four point, it signaled his passage into manhood and still ranked as one of his favorite memories.

"Erik, there you go daydreaming again," chided Ruby. "It looks like the weather's getting worse. I think we should leave."

"You always were the worrier of the Johnson clan," replied her brother. "We'll be okay."

"Even after hearing the severe weather advisory on the radio a thousand times while driving up here? I'm sorry, Erik. I'm going to wait in the car where it's safe."

"Okay, Sis. See you later."

As Ruby fought her way across the parking lot through the gusty wind, Erik's eyes misted over as he thought back to his many trips to the Kinzua Bridge with his father, Paul. They especially loved to come here to fly balsa wood airplanes they made from kits bought at Ruth Brothers' Hardware in Bradford. It took days to glue together the pieces and cover the wings and fuselages with tissue paper. After all that work, they glided their planes from the bridge toward

Kushequa, knowing full well they'd never recover them from the thick forest below. The gliders had rubber band powered engines and zoomed with the wind for miles until disappearing from sight.

"No wonder Dad wanted his ashes scattered over the Kinzua Valley," sighed Erik, as the treasured recollection drifted back into his subconscious.

Erik left the visitors' information stand and trudged toward the railroad tracks leading onto the Kinzua Viaduct. While he tramped along, he could hear his Uncle Dick's voice in his head telling how the bridge came to be built.

"When General Thomas Kane returned from leading his Bucktail Regiment in the Civil War," Dick lectured, "he found his land in McKean County brimming with coal. With Buffalo, New York, using over three million tons of coal a year, Kane needed to find a way to carry his product to market. To accomplish this, he founded the New York, Lake Erie, and Western Railroad and began laying track to the north. To get to Buffalo, he could either take a six mile detour around the Kinzua Valley or build this bridge. Kane decided to span the gorge when he learned how big a pile of greenbacks that would save. The general also wanted to overcome the challenge of building the world's highest bridge. He then contacted the brilliant engineer Octave Chanute, who gave the bid to the Phoenixville Bridge Works. The rest, as they say, is history."

Johnson marched forward cradling his father's burial urn. He was unaware of the tears streaming down his face until a fierce wind smacked him as he proceeded onto the bridge walkway. The structure swayed and bucked beneath his feet until he found it increasingly difficult to maintain his balance. With a grim smile, Erik remembered the stories of such winds ripping the tops off boxcars and blowing whole cargoes of hemlock bark from the trains. That was why engine speeds were regulated to five miles an hour when they chugged across the trestle.

As Erik inched along holding tightly to the railing, he recalled the time he and his dad were trapped here by a train. When the locomotive rumbled onto the bridge, the swaying of the tracks intensified, causing Paul's face to go pale. Visibly shaken, the elder Johnson straddled a railing post and let his feet dangle off the bridge. He wedged Erik against the post and wrapped his powerful arms around him while the long string of coal cars jarred every bone in their bodies. After the train had rattled past, Paul stood and vomited over the railing. That was the only time the boy had seen his dad frightened. It wasn't until years later that Erik learned how Paul nearly fell from the roof of a round house that serviced train engines in Bradford. Since his boyhood in the 1930's, Paul successfully had hid his fear of heights until again faced by sudden danger in a very high place.

Erik fought his way across the bridge until he could see the rain-swollen Kinzua Creek below him through the patchy mist. Gripping the urn in the crook of his arm, Johnson loosened the lid and said a final prayer for his father's soul. Afterward, he launched Paul's ashes into the wind and watched them blow violently off toward Kushequa.

The wind had now reached gale proportions, and it was all Erik could do to hang onto the railing. Fearfully, he stared across the valley at the leafy July woods that obscured the rocky terrain. It had been no problem for the builders to quarry sandstone blocks from the neighboring hills, he remembered. These were cut into stone piers and buried thirty-five feet into the ground to anchor the iron legs of the viaduct.

"Too bad the original anchor bolts weren't replaced when the bridge was rebuilt," muttered Erik, feeling the violent sway of the structure beneath him. "Those rusty bolts were the major concern that ended train traffic last year."

Johnson dropped to his knees and began crawling toward the park end of the bridge. It took every ounce of strength he could muster to fight the wind assailing him. The sky had turned the color of hard-boiled egg yolks and churned violently. When the wind swirled with tornado intensity, Erik clung desperately to the railing and watched the trees scalped from the hills. It was the last sight he remembered as the railing broke loose, hurling him into the abyss.

Erik extended his arms and legs and floated like a sky diver toward Grant's Rocks. The air was alive with singing shards of metal and splinters of wood. He closed his eyes to keep the wind from plucking them out and heard the bridge fight for its life behind him.

Erik glided along with the wind until he was rocked by a violent collision that sent a sudden numbness through him. Opening his eyes, he found himself immersed in murky light. He felt someone grip his hand. He turned to find his father floating beside him, looking thirty-five again. Paul was dressed in his black and red deer hunting clothes. A broad grin stretched across his face as he pointed toward a glowing tunnel opening through the clouds ahead.

RALPH CROSSMIRE HATES MY FACE

Fear glittered in Millie Little's dark, close-set eyes when Lu, the staff manager, told her her assignment. Millie had only begun volunteering yesterday and venturing to the other end of the spooky Old Jail Museum operated by the McKean County Historical Society filled her with dread. She knew her fate was sealed, though, when Lu added with an encouraging smile, "Yes, doing research in the library will be the perfect job for a retired teacher like you."

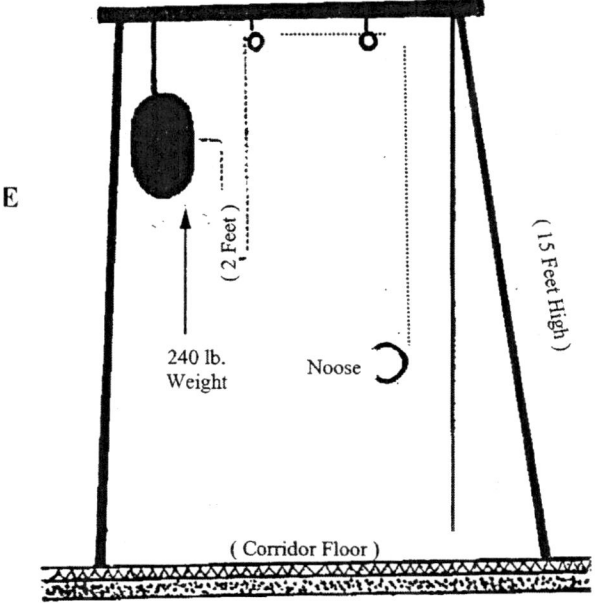

Millie shuddered when she closed the office door and entered the dank foyer. There, her attention was drawn to a grim display of the death machine used to hang murderers in the 1890's. In a locked glass case, manacles and leg chains sat alongside actual nooses used to choke the life out of men who had been incarcerated within these very walls.

"M-m-maybe their spirits still lurk here," stammered Millie, as she stared irresistibly up the long stairwell that ran next to the hangman exhibit. After glancing with dread at the yawning apartment door above, she added, "And maybe I should go to work before my imagination gets the best of me."

Mrs. Little scurried through the gift shop and entered a hall next to the jail museum. Millie had been given a wonderful tour there last evening and saw priceless artifacts, old weapons, and Civil War memorabilia. Although no one was in the museum, the light was still on and glinted through the bars of the cell door securing the area. Being an ex-teacher also made Millie very responsible, so she stepped up to the switch and clicked it off.

"No use wasting energy," she muttered. "I'm sure the historical society's on a very limited budget."

Darkness no sooner spread through the museum when the light again flicked on of its own volition. With a startled gasp, Millie jumped back and then reached again to turn off the switch. This time as she touched it, a violent shock passed through her fingers and knocked her halfway across the hall. Reeling, she shrieked for all she was worth until Lu came rushing to assist her.

"What happened?" panted the office manager. "Are you okay?"

"That light switch zapped me!" yelped Mrs. Little, pointing toward the opposite wall.

"You mean this one?" asked Lu, snapping the switch.

"Hey, the light stayed off. H-h-how did you do that?"

"Now, calm down, Millie. This building spooks a lot of people until they get used to it. Do you want to lie down for a while? We have a sofa in the board room."

"N-n-o-o, I'm all right. All I need is to get cracking on that research. Reading always makes me feel better."

"Okay, see you later."

Lu patted Millie reassuringly on the shoulder and then returned to the office to finish a press release. After she had gone, Mrs. Little stepped into the corridor leading to the lecture hall. With trepidation, she passed another set of steps that rose to the right into the craft room on the second floor. Millie had just drawn even with the stairwell when a man's voice demanded, "Who's there?"

Jumping a foot in the air, Millie squeaked, "Your new volunteer, sir. Can I help you with anything?"

"C-o-m-e h-e-r-e," droned the voice in a creepy tone that made Millie's flesh crawl. "Now!"

Mrs. Little backed away from the stairs as a very dark feeling crept over her. Whirling, she fled through the lecture room, around the corner, and on into the library in the far wing of the building. Only after she was surrounded by bunkers of books did she break into tears.

Millie sobbed and trembled, trembled and sobbed. Finally, she produced a lace handkerchief from the sleeve of her blouse and daubed at her dainty features.

When she had composed herself, she shuffled through the card catalog to locate books about the Great Depression. Afterward, she dragged a whole armful of dusty tomes from the surrounding shelves and placed them on the desk. Settling into a padded chair, she was soon immersed in some very fascinating reading.

Time passed happily for Millie as she continued her research. She had just delved into FDR's New Deal when she heard a series of steady thumps reverberating from the lecture hall. The nearer the thumps came, the more they resembled heavy footsteps. Then, she heard a man's voice rumble, "If you won't come to me, I'll come for you!"

The chilling words sent adrenaline shooting through Millie's veins. Snatching up her purse, she feverishly ransacked it as the footsteps tromped closer and closer and closer and closer. It wasn't until the incessant clopping was a few yards away that she fished out the nail file that had eluded her. Brandishing her weapon, she leaped from the chair and rushed to slam the door just as the footfalls reached it. Impelled by panic, she whipped the door closed with all her might. Only after she shot home the bolt with a loud snick, did she hear the sound of receding wind followed by utter silence.

Millie leaned panting against the door for the longest time. When her pulse finally slowed to normal, she creaked open the library door and peered into the empty hall. It was now midday, and the sun streamed through the windows to warm and cheer her. Finally, looking neither left nor right, she streaked for the safety of the Old Jail office.

When Millie tore into the gift shop, she nearly knocked down Mrs. Freeman, the historical society president. Mrs. F. was restocking the shelves with books by local authors, and she spilled an armful of ghost story anthologies on the floor. While righting herself, the president finally croaked, "You're running like Old Nick is after you, dear. What's wrong?"

"I-I-I've been hearing things," stammered Millie. "T-t-they scare me. . ."

"What kind of things?"

"V-v-voices. F-f-footsteps."

"Oh, that's just Ralph Crossmire," laughed Mrs. Freeman with a relieved sigh. "He's our resident spook. He won't hurt you."

"Oh, yeah?"

"Yeah. He just plays harmless pranks to let us know he's around."

"Sure, like the time Ralph took my keys," chuckled Lu, coming from the office to join the conversation. "I had laid them in the middle of my desk, and they simply disappeared. I flew into a panic and tore the place apart looking for them. I shouldn't have bothered because Ralph returned them later that afternoon. I found the keys just before closing time dangling from a lamp near the door."

"I-I-I d-d-don't believe he's harmless," cried Millie, snatching a comb from her purse to nervously groom her old-fashioned hairdo and part it down the middle.

"The worst thing I remember him doing was taking a photo of the 1930 Port A. baseball team from a locked display case," countered Mrs. Freeman. "Even that picture showed up later perched atop the fire alarm system in the basement."

"If he's not bent on revenge, then why does this Ralph Crossmire haunt the Old Jail?" gulped Millie, still not convinced.

"He was hung here in 1893 for killing his mother," answered Lu. "Of course, a lot of folks, including the sheriff, thought he was innocent. Come on, now, enough of this talk. Why don't we go next door, and I'll give you a job that will take your mind off everything? We'll be right here if you need us. Okay?"

"I-I-I guess so if you promise not to leave for lunch, or anything."

"Sure."

Lu led Millie into the feature room where several New Deal bulletin boards were taking shape. There were half-filled display cases there, too, and a naked mannequin. Pointing toward the mannequin, the office manager said, "We're portraying this fellow as a CCC man. Why don't you get him ready for work? His clothes are in that box."

"T-t-that'll be fun," sniffed Mrs. Little. "I had enough Cub Scout sons to dress in my day, so this should be right up my alley."

"Good. Now, remember. Eileen and I are just next door."

Millie pulled a kaki shirt, kaki pants, a campaign hat, and a pair of clodhoppers from the box at the mannequin's feet. Inspecting the clothing, she said, "It's so nice to feel useful again. I-I-I just couldn't sit home after Harry died. Despite my earlier scare, this is much better."

Mrs. Little hummed an uplifting hymn as she pulled the shirt over the dummy's torso and buttoned it. She had just begun to yank on his pants when one-by-one the shirt buttons popped open. In the next instant the campaign hat levitated from the floor and settled on the CCC man's head. When the boots sprang to life and began kicking her mercilessly, she wailed in pain and terror and ran in circles with the clodhoppers hot on her heels. "Stop, Ralph Crossmire," she pleaded. "Leave me alone!"

Finally, Millie's brain told her to flee, so she careened down the hall past the museum. She no sooner drew even with the barred entrance when the museum lights flashed on and off until they assumed a strobe effect. It was then that the familiar, creepy voice bellowed from the bowels of the locked room, "Here. I'm here. I'm here! I'm h-e-r-e!" As the voice reached a horrible crescendo, Millie forgot all about the pain shooting through her bruised legs.

Disoriented by the noise and pulsing light, Mrs. Little tottered for the entrance of the Old Jail. Wild-eyed, she burst into the foyer and clawed furiously at the main door until Eileen and Lu dashed from the gift shop to restrain her.

"Why, you're absolutely frantic, dear," gasped Mrs. Freeman. "Please. Come sit down."

"Yes, calm yourself," cried Lu. "We're here to help. And listen."

With tears streaming down her thin, pretty face, Millie allowed herself to be escorted into a comfortable chair behind an oak desk in the office. She pursed her full lips and then blubbered, "Ralph k-k-kicked me!"

"Kicked you?" echoed Eileen. "That can't be. He doesn't bother any of us."

"Then, look at how black and blue I am!" screeched Mrs. Little indignantly. "I suppose I imagined my contusions, too!"

"Maybe this will shed some light on the matter," said Lu, handing Millie a booklet produced by the historical society. "Why don't you read about the Crossmire case? We spent months researching it. Learning the truth can alleviate a person's fear."

Mrs. Little laid the booklet on the desk and madly scanned its pages, while Lu and Eileen hovered over her shoulder. She hadn't read long before she snapped, "I told you Ralph isn't harmless! It says here Nettie Crossmire was strangled and then bludgeoned to death with a stout piece of wood. What sort of monster would murder his mother like that?"

"But the evidence against Ralph was circumstantial," objected Mrs. Freeman, squeezing the agitated volunteer's hand. "There were no witnesses, and he was working in Mt. Jewett at the time."

"Oh, yeah? Let me read further, so I can make up my own mind."

Mrs. Little turned the page, and her eyes lit upon a sketch that made her blanch with horror. Leaping from her chair, she shrieked, "Now, I know why Ralph Crossmire hates my face!"

"Why's that?" mumbled Lu.

"Because I look just like Nettie!"

MARY AND EMMETT

Mary led her husband Emmett to the couch. With the condescending tone reserved for a pet, she commanded him to sit. Mumbling vaguely to himself, the shriveled old man plopped onto the cushions and fixed his empty gaze on the television screen opposite him. *The Jetsons* were on, not that it really made much difference.

The old woman patted her husband on the shoulder and then trundled off into the adjoining kitchenette to wash the breakfast dishes. As she stacked the plates and coffee cups into the dishwasher, she glanced periodically at Emmett to make sure he hadn't toppled off the couch like he'd done so many times lately. How hard it was for her to believe that just a year ago the same man had planted a garden, mowed the lawn, and trimmed weeds from the doorstep of their family home. But that was before the arteries had begun to harden in his brain. Now, about all he could do was feed himself. The box of diapers beneath the kitchen table testified to that.

Mary's face clouded as she reflected upon the difficult period of adjustment she had had since moving into the Oakhurst Space Age Apartment Complex for the Elderly. Her husband's condition had worsened dramatically in that span of five months, which necessitated her babysitting him twenty-four hours a day. Also, that same proud independence that had prevented the woman from placing Emmett in a nursing home, had kept her, at first, from accepting such time-saving conveniences as dishwashers, intercoms, self-changing beds, and robot attendants with which her new residence was fully equipped.

Mary was still grumbling about these "gadgets" as she shoveled Emmett's half-eaten scrambled egg breakfast down the garbage disposal. At the same time, she couldn't help marvel at the enormous capacity of those grinding disposal jaws that had once made short work of a giant, economy size bottle of detergent that had slipped from her grasp. She would never forget how the crunch of plastic, that had followed the bottle's plummet down the drain, had made her skin crawl.

A buzzer sounded above the old woman's head, and she tilted her wizened face toward the ceiling.

"Yes."

"Do. . .you. . .need. . .anything. . .at. . .the. . . supermarket. . .today. . .Mrs. Gray?" droned a mechanical voice from a concealed speaker.

"No thank you."

"You. . . are. . . welcome."

Another buzzer sounded, and Mary opened the dishwasher to find her plates and cups sparkling clean. She soon became so absorbed in restacking them in the cupboard that she didn't notice Emmett, his face beaming like a mischievous child, get to his feet and tiptoe across the carpet. At that moment an exhaust fan switched on automatically to clear the air of steam rising from her dishes. Its steady roar completely concealed the closing of the front door. It was another ten minutes before Mary turned from cleaning the kitchen sink to find the sofa empty.

"Emmett? You know I hate playing hide-and-seek. Come out, come out, wherever you are!"

As expected, there was no reply, so the old woman went through her daily ritual of checking behind the couch, in the closets, and under the beds. Emmett was not to be found in any of those hiding places, but Mary was still unconcerned. With a triumphant smile she charged into the bathroom and flung open the shower curtain. When she found the stall empty, she hastened into the living room and pressed the intercom buzzer.

"Emmett's escaped again!" she shouted into the contraption. "You'll need to go fetch him."

"Yes. . .Mrs. Gray."

For half-an-hour Mary paced nervously back and forth across the carpet, biting her fingernails to the quick. Finally, there was a knock on the door, and two robot attendants ushered Emmett into the living room. The old man glanced warily from one of his captors to the other. He mumbled incoherently until his wife stepped forward and took him firmly by the ear.

"You're a bad boy," scolded Mary. "Look at the trouble you've caused these. . .er. . ."

Mary paused uncertainly as she regarded the humanoid figures that towered over her. Dressed in their bright blue uniforms, they would have almost passed for real security guards if it had not been for their clear, plastic, dome-like heads.

"May. . .I. . .suggest. . .that. . .you. . .keep. . .your. .door. . .locked," droned the first robot while he bowed from the room.

"May. . .I. . .suggest. . .that. . .you. . .mind. . .your. .own. . .business," mocked the old woman, hooking the security chain behind them. "Come on, Emmett, it's time for your morning shave."

Mary retained her firm grip on Emmett's ear and led him into the bathroom. She had just removed his undershirt and lathered up his face when a buzzer announced another visitor. With a curse, she stormed into the foyer and ripped open the front door to find the robot postman waiting with the morning mail. She had little time to examine it, however, before the garbled strains of "Mary Had a Little Lamb" had her scurrying for the bathroom. When she peeked breathlessly inside, there was Emmett, still dressed in his pants and best shoes, splashing and laughing in the shower. Naturally, he had forgotten to draw the plastic curtain, and the automatic drain strained with a deafening screech to channel off the water gushing onto the tile floor. By the time Mary had retrieved Emmett from the shower, had shaved him, and had set him to work with a mop, the old wife was soaked and on the verge of tears.

The mid-afternoon sun filtered through the drawn living room curtains, highlighting the paleness of Mary's cheeks. The old woman rested in an overstuffed chair with a damp rag plastered on her forehead. The apartment was much too stuffy for her liking, but it seemed to have an anesthetizing effect on Emmett, who was stretched out dozing on the couch. Mary became oblivious to the heat watching her husband's toothless mouth form little *O's* of snoring. Soon, her head slouched forward on her chest, and she was sound asleep.

When Mary woke, the room was completely dark. Although she could no longer hear or see Emmett, it wasn't hard to pinpoint his position by the faint but distinct odor that wafted across the room. Mary flicked on the lamp beside her chair and was greeted by a disgusting sight. There lay her husband face-up on the sofa hugging a pillow and sucking his thumb. He must have gotten too warm during his sleep, for now his trousers dangled from one leg onto the floor. His diaper had been ripped open, and telltale custard-color stains covered the cushions beneath him. There were similar stains smeared on the tails of his white shirt.

"Emmett Gray! Get up this instant!"

The old man jerked awake, and a custard-colored hand appeared from beneath him to wipe sleep from his eyes. With a shriek, Mary leaped forward and took Emmett by the ear. She jerked him to his feet and led him kicking and bawling into the bathroom. He tripped on his trousers that still dangled from one leg and fell with a splat on the padded floor of the shower stall. Mary drew the plastic curtain and turned on the shower full blast. Emmett sputtered as a sheet of cold water hit him square in the face.

"You lather up good, you hear?" hissed Mary as she tossed the old man a bar of soap. "I'm going to get you a clean change of clothes, so don't you dare leave this bathroom."

Mary returned moments later and commanded her husband to strip. While he handled his shirt and pants through the shower curtain, a noxious odor made the old woman gag. She turned, holding her breath, and stuffed the vile garments through the clothes chute near the sink. For once she was thankful that the robot laundry did all of her washing.

When Emmett was showered and freshly dressed, Mary led him by the hand to the small table that divided the living room from the kitchenette. Then, she sat him down and went to fetch some eggs and bacon from the refrigerator. In a matter of minutes she prepared a fluffy omelet that she heaped onto Emmett's plate. With thoughts of shampooing the sofa clouding her face, Mary finally collapsed opposite her husband to watch him eat.

Emmett sank his fork into the steaming platter of eggs but did not lift it to his mouth. He was plain sick of eggs. That was about all that lady ever fixed him. Making choo choo noises, he dug a tunnel through the center of the omelet instead.

Mary reached across the table and gave the old man a light slap on the hand. "Don't play with your food," she snapped.

Like a spoiled child, Emmett threw down his fork and then hurled his plate onto the floor. Instantly, Mary leaped up and aimed a blow at her husband's head. At the last second her clenched fist veered past his ear and came thudding down on the table.

"Look at all the food you've wasted!" screeched Mary, nursing her bruised hand. "And look at that mess! Now, I'll have to feed your meal to the garbage disposal. Now—"

Suddenly, a malicious smile flickered across Mary's lips as she envisioned that giant, economy size bottle of detergent disappearing down the drain. She turned to flip on the exhaust fan. When she once more faced her husband, all the thunder had faded from her brow.

"Come over here to the sink, Emmett," she cooed below the roar of the fan. "There's something here you can play with. . ."

THE GOLDENROD

Jacob Martin cut loose with a vile string of epitaphs as he swatted at a flight of bees that dive-bombed him from his blind side. It was sweltering hot for the twenty-third of September, and the afternoon sun glinted on a row of red lumps that sprouted atop the paunchy man's bald head. When he shifted his scythe from one sweaty paw to the other, the fresh bee stings made him wince with pain.

The fat man swore again. He was standing chest-deep in a sea of goldenrod that sprouted from the earth where his once bountiful garden had flourished. A continuous gaudy wave of weeds now stretched from the very steps of his porch to the distant hills aglow with crimson oaks. This was the third time in as many weeks that he had hewed a new path to his dog kennel located in the center of his backyard. The very thought of this annoyance threw Martin into another sudden fit of labor. With an anger oblivious to heat or pain, he hacked away at the arrow-straight stalks that hemmed him in. Ironically, the scythe was his only gardening tool that wasn't caked with rust.

A half-hour later, an exhausted Jacob Martin chased off another swarm of attacking bees just as he reached the dog pen. With trembling fingers, he unlocked the gate and collapsed inside. He lay panting in the dirt until old Duke, his prize beagle, waddled from the kennel to lick his flushed cheeks. Jacob threw his arms around the hound and wheezed, "Thank God I made it to you, boy."

Outside the steel mesh enclosure, a shudder passed through the goldenrod. Saw-edged leaves wigwagged silent messages, and waving plumes of flower heads, heavy with insects, bent toward the pen as if in an attitude of listening. What resulted was the same faint rustling buzz that had kept the man tossing night after night in his bed. He recognized it instantly and huddled even closer to Duke. Strangely, there wasn't even a whisper of a breeze.

Jacob could feel the sun burn through his tightly closed eyelids as he pondered with growing fear an enigma that had haunted him since spring. What still mystified him were the amazing regenerative powers of the goldenrod army that had invaded his property. He knew from research in the town library that the scientific name for the goldenrod was Solidago from the Latin "solidare," meaning to make whole. The plants were so-called because of their reputed curative powers. Until they had grown to five-foot in height in a week's time, he had always assumed that these curative powers referred to their potential benefit to the human species.

The only human to whom Jacob had dared confide this enigma was his neighbor, Aaron Shotts. Aaron was another gardening fanatic and had watched with alarm as the goldenrod spread in an almost calculated series of maneuvers from the foot of the distant hills to subjugate first his potato patch and then his prize-winning rose garden. Consequently, he had gladly joined forces with Jacob for a counterattack against the Solidago.

Jacob shook his head in wonderment while recalling the neighbors' attempt to annihilate their adversary. They had used a pesticide that he had never known to fail even on the most resilient strain of dandelion, and predictably the treated weeds shriveled and died. There was little time for celebration, however, for within two weeks a hardier army of goldenrod had sprung up to reclaim the garden plots. Upon its resurgence, the old men were shocked to learn that it now thrived upon the very pesticide that had previously choked it out. Some of the plants sprang up to six-foot in height. More shocking still, the bees also grew to gigantic proportions. The droning of these insects continued twenty-four hours a day as they feasted gluttonously upon their hosts.

Suddenly, Duke stiffened. The rustling of the goldenrod increased to a deafening level, but somehow the sound went undetected by the man huddled beside him. The hairs bristled on the hound's back, and he growled a low warning before disappearing tail-first into his kennel. Despite his master's repeated coaxing, the dog remained cowering within.

Finally, Jacob staggered to his feet and stumbled from the protective walls of the dog pen. His heart fluttered uncertainly, and his head ached from his recent labor and the heat. When he found the path he had just blazed overgrown with even taller goldenrod, he began to question his own sanity.

Lunging forward in desperation, Jacob grabbed the nearest plants and attempted to uproot them with brute strength. He yelped and immediately withdrew his hands. Staring numbly at his left palm, he saw a jagged cut bisecting his lifeline.

The rustling of the saw-toothed leaves grew more violent still and blended with the buzzing of pollen-glutted insects. The sun glinted mockingly from the disk and ray florets. The earth began to spin beneath the man's feet as the gaudy plants towered over his head. Then, there was nothing but cool silence.

Aaron Shotts dozed fitfully at his writing desk and then woke with a start. Was that a scream or just his sodden brain playing tricks on him? Aaron leaned back in his chair to stretch his knotted shoulder muscles. Because he hadn't slept much in over a month, his face was now a mere caricature of its former self. His eyes were sunken and lusterless. His mouth drooped idiotically.

A faint rustle passed through the open window, and the old man glanced warily at the lengthening shadows spreading across his den. After noting the blood red reflection of the late evening sun dancing on the wall, he mumbled, "Maybe I'd better go see how Jacob made out with his path-clearing project."

Aaron stamped woodenly across the yard that separated his split-level home from Jacob's identical residence. When a shudder passed through the sea of yellow flower heads bobbing in the backyard, he spotted a few single goldenrod stalks sprouting from his otherwise well-trimmed side yard. *Funny,* he thought, *those weren't there yesterday.* Quickening his pace, he made a mental note to return and uproot the pesky plants before they could choke out the grass between the houses, as well.

The lanky old man climbed onto his neighbor's front porch and rang the doorbell. An ominous buzz echoed briefly through the house. After several minutes' wait, Aaron rang it again. This time the hum did not cease when he removed his finger from the button. Finally, he creaked open the door and called, "Jacob. Jacob? Are you —"

Aaron's voice strangled with terror when he found the living room transformed into a hive of buzzing insects. His eyes were drawn from the open window that admitted a steady stream of pollen-laden bees to the hexagonal patterns of honeycomb that encrusted the four walls and ceiling. It was then that he first heard the low, almost human howl emitting from the backyard.

Aaron backed down the porch steps without closing the door. Then, he bolted around the corner of the house and plunged neck-deep into the goldenrod jungle. As he thrashed toward the distant dog pen, the goldenrod stalks sprang to an even greater height in his wake. If his neighbor had cut a path earlier that afternoon, there was no evidence of it now.

The air was so heavy with pollen that Aaron's breathing came in rattling gasps by the time he had reached his objective. What he found just outside the steel mesh enclosure was enough to stifle his breathing altogether. There, beneath a swarm of feasting bees, lay Jacob Martin, his big bald head tilted back against the fence. It didn't take any coroner to tell he was dead. His vacant eyes stared skyward in the most ghastly fashion, and there was a hint of yellow powder around the corners of his mouth. The powder was the exact color of the flower heads that towered over the corpse. Conversely, the flesh of the dead man's face was the dull, bluish shade of a strangulation victim.

A shiver passed through Aaron as the sun set behind the distant oak-ridden hills. There was another sudden howl followed by a sharper rustling of the goldenrod.

BAD THINGS HAPPEN TO BAD MEN

"Where's Ellen's alimony check?" snarled the lawyer's voice in Dylan March's ear. "She's had it with your procrastination crap!"

"And I'm sick of her bitchery," muttered Dylan into the phone. "Isn't divorce supposed to end a couple's misery? In every religion I've heard of, there's life after death."

"Always the wise guy, aren't you, pal?"

"Yeah, even with a hangover," replied March, grabbing his throbbing forehead.

"Well, wise guy, this is what's going down. You will either have Ellen's check by Friday, or my associates will confiscate your photography equipment for me. What they'll do for their own pleasure is another matter."

"You can't do that!"

"Bad things happen to bad men."

"But that'd ruin my livelihood. Then, how will I pay anything?"

"By finally growing up and getting a real job. As I see it, that's the only way Ellen will ever get what's coming to her."

"The bloodsucker already has the house, the camp, and the bank account. What more can she want, the proverbial pound of flesh?"

"I'm not listening to any more of this!" barked the lawyer. "By Friday! Understand? After a little arm twisting, your agent gladly told me how to locate you. There'll be no weaseling out of your obligation this time!"

Before Dylan could answer, a loud click reverberated in his head. He let the cell phone slip from his fingers and fall to the worn rug. Exhaling a low sigh, he flopped back into bed to watch the sun set behind the neon GET_YS_URG MOT_L sign. He had somehow lost a whole day, and he knew his bacon was really fried this time.

"Shouldn't have stayed out 'til beer-thirty chasin' skirts," March groaned. "Hell, I missed the big cavalry reenactment I was sent here to photograph for *Blue and Gray Magazine*. Fat chance the 'zine will pay my expenses now. And what about the grand I owe Bitchzilla? I better come up with a way to make a few thou or blow this dive quick!"

Dylan rolled over and covered his head with a lumpy pillow. His temples pounded with the effort, and his stomach churned mightily. He hadn't lain still for more than a minute when he knew he would be sick. Staggering into the bathroom, he bent over the toilet just in time to retch and gag horribly. A bout of the dry heaves followed until he was too spent to worry about anything other than returning to bed. In the end it was easier to collapse on the floor. He hardly felt the coldness of the tile when he crumpled up near the sink.

The next thing Dylan remembered was an urgent poking and the breathy whispers of "You all right, mister? Mister? Mister?"

The photographer's eyes popped open to find a frightened maid bent over him. He almost laughed aloud when he saw her garish orange apron and yellow rubber gloves. Her hair reminded him of cat's fur. It stuck out every which way from beneath her polka dot kerchief.

"My sugar's actin' up again," lied March, crawling groggily to his feet. "That's why I passed out. What time is it, anyhow?"

"Time to quit boozin'," replied the maid, fanning her hand in front of her nose.

"No, really. What time is it?"

"Ten a.m. Checkout's in an hour."

"Not for me. I have reservations 'til Saturday. What are you doin' in here, anyway? I didn't think you cleaned occupied rooms."

"I do when they turn into pigstys."

"Start out in the bedroom then, will ya? 'Til I get spruced up."

"You could begin by brushing them teeth," replied the maid, again waving her hand in front of her nose.

Dylan shooed the protesting woman from the bathroom and slammed the door behind her. *Which one of the Lee sisters is she?* he wondered. *Ug Lee or Home Lee?*

"You better hurry up in there," yelled the maid. "I got work to do."

"Yeah! Yeah!"

Bending over the sink, the photographer splashed some cold water on his face and then ran a comb through his wavy, blond hair. *I still got it,* he thought, examining his boyish features in the mirror. *Not a barfly alive would suspect I was pushing forty. Who needs Viagra when he flows like Niagara?*

Just to aggravate the maid, March took his time shaving. He could hear her in the next room muttering to herself as she changed the bed sheets. After slapping on a healthy dose of aftershave, he swaggered out of the bathroom and shouted to the woman, "It's all yours, mama. Knock yourself out."

Dylan strutted into the motel lounge and fed two quarters and a dime into the Coke machine. "Ah-h-h," he said after opening the can. "The breakfast of derelicts."

The photographer plopped into a soft recliner and snatched *The Gettysburg Times* from a coffee table. Ignoring the grim news from Iraq splashed across the front page, he turned directly to the entertainment section. After checking out which bands were playing at the local bars, he strayed across the headline, "Reenactors Needed for Video Shoot."

With excitement gleaming in his eyes, Dylan read aloud: "Attention, Civil War reenactors. American Talent's latest winner, Sherry Silver, will be in Gettysburg on Friday, July 10th, to shoot her first music video. Union soldiers are needed as extras for this event. Extras will be chosen from 4-6 p.m. Thursday, July 9th at the Gettysburg Wax Museum. Uniform authenticity is a must."

"Hot damn!" exclaimed Dylan. "How much would *Star Magazine* pay for professional photos of that shoot? I'll get right on it."

Dylan scrambled out the door and bolted down Steinwehr Avenue to the sutler's shop he remembered was only a block away. When he arrived, he found the place packed with a rabid mob of jostling customers. With all the good clothes long gone, fat men tried to squeeze into small Union jackets, tall fellows struggled with high-water trousers, and scrawny guys rifled the kids' section. As the photographer reached to grab the last blue sack coat dangling on a long, empty rack, a desperate wannabe reenactor pushed him aside and snarled, "That's mine!"

"What do you mean, yours?" yelped March, grabbing the left sleeve. "Gimme it!"

The two men played tug-of-war with the disputed coat, nearly ripping it in half. They pushed and yanked and yanked and cursed until a clerk burst from behind the cash resister like a perturbed hen. "Shame on you," she clucked, slapping the combatants with a long broom. "Ever since the American Talent people came to town, everyone's gone mad."

Dylan ducked to escape the blow aimed at his head. At the same instant, the coat slipped out of his grasp. His rival went flying into a group of customers gathered at the belt counter. This caused another ruckus, and the beleaguered clerk charged off leveling her room like a musket.

Still sweating from his skirmish, Dylan circled the shop to search for the other gear he would need to portray a Union soldier. He soon discovered that no blue kepis remained on the hat racks and that just gray canteens dangled from pegs near the cash register. The only brogans remaining were size six, and they were marked up to double the normal price.

The photographer swore in frustration. He was about to leave the madhouse when he noticed a rack of white dusters jammed in a corner. Above them hung a wide assortment of straw hats. A smile flickered across his lips when he saw the dusters. Nonchalantly, he crossed the room and began trying them on until he found one that fit. As luck would have it, the first straw hat he grabbed was just his size.

"Oh, so now you're goin' for a buggy ride?" jeered the fellow he had fought for the sack coat.

"Sure," lied Dylan. "Anything's better than hassling with you maniacs."

The photographer pushed his way to the cash register and breathed a sigh of relief when his purchases cleared on his nearly maxed-out credit card. Hustling through the door, he ran down the street to a hardware store. There, he purchased a saw, a brush, four 2x2's, plywood, wood glue, and a quart of brown latex paint. These items also were under his credit limit, so he returned to the motel with his arms full and his head swimming with happy plans.

At three-thirty that afternoon, Dylan climbed in his rented Olds and roared off to the Wax Museum. By the time he arrived, the parking lot was jammed with reenactors who strutted about showing off their authentic gear. There were Zouaves in baggy red pants, an assortment of blue-coated infantry, and even a few Bucktail skirmishers with Sharps rifles slung over their shoulders. The most awesome of all, though, was the troop of Yankee cavalry. Dressed like the gaudy General Custer's men, they came clattering up the street on their mounts waving their sabers and howling "Charge!" Their dramatics were wasted because the American Talent director, Mr. Frank, didn't arrive in his silver Mercedes until after the cavalry had cantered into the lot and dismounted.

As soon as Dylan spotted the director, he leaped out of his car and pulled an old-fashioned camera mounted on a tripod from the backseat. Using the tripod as a weapon, he fought his way through the mob to the registration table. By then, the director had chosen some Iron Brigade reenactors and Custer's cavalry for the shoot.

"Who might you be portraying?" asked Mr. Frank when he spied March in his long, white duster and straw hat.

"Alexander Gardner. He was the photographer who shot many famous photos of the Gettysburg Battle. No Civil War video would be complete without a member of the 1860's news media present."

"But we don't allow cameras on the location," Frank said.

"This isn't a real camera," assured Dylan. "Although it's an exact replica of the one that took tintype photos, it isn't functional. I should know. I built it this morning."

"Okay. You're hired. I'll need your name for the payroll."

"I'm Dylan March. Where and when do I report, sir?"

"The video shoot's at the Devil's Den. It will begin promptly at ten a.m. Be there an hour early."

"Why, isn't that appropriate," Dylan beamed.

"What do you mean?" asked the director.

"Alexander Gardner's most famous photo was of a dead Rebel sharpshooter at that very location. See you at nine o'clock."

"Here's your pass, March. You'll need it to get through security."

"Thanks!"

Suppressing his glee, the photographer went directly back to the motel and had a quiet dinner in the lounge. Instead of the usual Tom Collins, he ordered a tall glass of ice tea with his rare steak. He chewed his food mechanically when it came. To calm his nerves, he looked out the window until the motel sign glowed to life at dusk.

With a smirk, Dylan dropped ten pennies and a worthless poker chip on the table for the waitress. Then, he strode back to his room and picked up the camera he had built. Screwing off the top, he installed his new Nikon inside, so that it would shoot through the front shutter of his replica. The Nikon was a state-of-the-art voice activated model that didn't require any button pushing to operate it.

"Now, I can take all the pics of hot Sherry Silver that I want," gloated March when he finished concealing his modern camera. "No one will suspect a thing."

Grinning craftily, Dylan returned to the lounge to learn the exact time. Afterward, he set his alarm clock and checked it twice before crawling into bed at ten o'clock. Only then did his excitement overspill, and he spent the night tossing and turning on the mattress. Winding himself in and out of his sheets, he kept muttering, "Got to get some shuteye. Big day tomorrow. Big day. Can't screw up again. Not again."

March's eyes popped open at the first squawk of the alarm. Springing out of bed, he scrambled into his reenactor's garb and charged into the bathroom to paste on a phony moustache and some sideburns. He also blackened his eyebrows to make them more prominent. As he slicked down his shock of blond hair, he chortled, "Gotta make myself pretty for Sherry Silver. I'll charm the pants right off her between takes."

Dylan snatched up his camera and ran out the door to his rental car. It took many turns of the key to fire up the Olds, and he cursed impatiently under his breath until the engine finally rolled over.

The photographer sped south through the sleepy village of Gettysburg and on down the length of Cemetery Ridge. He was too busy counting the dollars he was going to make to heed the monuments and cannon he passed along the way. He veered right into a shallow valley and then squealed left onto Crawford Avenue. He hadn't gone far before he encountered a roadblock set up by the American Talent security staff. March slowed to a stop, showed his pass to a tough looking guard, and then drove through to a jumble of rocks spilling down the hill to the right.

"Man!" said Dylan with a low whistle. "They didn't name this place the Devil's Den for nothing.

From the brochure I read, these rocks were a gathering place for huge, poisonous snakes. Locals claim that Indians had weird ceremonies here, too. Add the ghosts of the Yanks and Rebs killed during the battle, and I sure wouldn't want to be out here at night."

Another security guard directed Dylan into a parking space at the foot of the Devil's Den. Scrambling from his car, the photographer grabbed his camera and followed a company of Yankee reenactors around to the back of the labyrinth of rocks. There, he found a long stage built between two boulders. The American Talent logo was anchored at the back and obscured much of the rock wall behind it. Stacks of amplifiers rose on each end of the stage, while band equipment dominated the center. The musicians had just arrived and began an impromptu sound check to make sure their instruments were in tune and that the monitors were positioned correctly.

Dylan continued to gawk at the many preparations going on around him when Director Frank grabbed him by the arm and blared, "March, I want you to stand directly in front of the stage and pretend to shoot photos of the action. I've hired two other gents to portray Civil War reporters. They'll stand next to you and scribble notes when the video camera pans this way. That was a great idea you had to include the old-time media."

"Thank you," replied March, grinning broadly. "How are you going to involve the other reenactors?"

"The infantry will be hiding in the rocks, firing their weapons. The cavalry will make a dramatic charge at the end, but that will be shot later today at another part of the battlefield. Why, look! Miss Silver has arrived. I better go and make sure she understands her part in the action."

The director bustled onto the stage just as an attractive, buxom blond made her entrance. She was dressed in a long Civil War period dress and had her hair tucked beneath a crocheted snood. Wearing less eyeliner, she could have stepped right out of 1863.

Mr. Frank held a quick conference with Sherry and her band. Afterward, he positioned the Union infantry among the boulders and behind a stone wall. By then, two reenactors dressed in old-fashioned suits and derbies had joined Dylan in front of the stage. As the journalists fetched note pads and pencils from their pockets, the photographer scrambled to set up his camera directly in front of Miss Silver.

When the director returned to center stage, Dylan shouted up to him, "Excuse me, sir. Shouldn't those be Rebel snipers over there among the rocks? According to history, Confederates held this position."

"Our video is for the teen market," replied Frank smugly. "What do kids care about history?"

The director had no sooner spoken when he appeared to trip over his own feet. Stumbling dangerously across the stage, he crashed into a stack of amplifiers before righting himself.

"Who pushed me?" Frank bellowed, whirling around to confront Sherry's bass player.

"Not me, man," squeaked the musician, flushing with embarrassment.

"Well, somebody did! Get ready. We're about to roll."

The director motioned with his hand, and three video cameras were pushed in on dollies to cover all angles of the set. Another camera was focused on the Union soldiers hiding about the Devil's Den. When all were situated, the director yelled, "Quiet! Take One! Action!"

On cue, Sherry Silver stepped up to the microphone and bowed her head over it. Her band, meanwhile, began a somber introduction complete with a funeral drumroll. This went on for a full thirty seconds as the vocalist prayed for a lover killed in combat. Blinking back real tears, she murmured in conclusion, "But I won't go on mourning, remembering the heat of your embrace."

Just as Silver finished her spiel, the musicians blasted into a furious rock assault, complete with screeching guitar. While the drummer pummeled his kit like a man possessed, the bassist thumped on his instrument until the Devil's Den shook with the flailing beat. As the music reached its crescendo, Sherry wailed licentiously and ripped off her prim dress. Beneath was a skintight velvet blue bikini that caused Dylan to drool so much he almost forgot to order his camera to snap photos.

The vocalist moaned as much as she sang. She just began an oversexed devil dance when the bass amp exploded with a thunderous crack. In an instant, the stage billowed with noxious smoke, sending the band scurrying for the wings.

"Cut! Cut!" howled the director. "Get a fire extinguisher. Quick!"

Sherry squealed at the top of her lungs until Dylan rushed forward, leaped onto the stage, and led her to safety. "Calm down, darlin'," he pleaded, stroking her bare shoulders. "Calm down before you strain those precious vocal chords."

"Get away from me, you creep!" screamed the singer when she felt Dylan's hand fondling her bosom.

"But Sherry, b-b-baby!" cooed Dylan. "Is that a way to treat your hero?"

"*Zero* is more like it! Security! Escort this creep back into the pit where he belongs."

With feigned indignity, March leaped off the stage before the guards reached him. Returning to his camera, he took a few shots of the bedlam caused by the explosion. It took a half-hour to extinguish the fire, calm everyone's nerves, and replace the damaged equipment. Sherry also had to be redressed and reassured. By the time order was restored, the sun had risen to where it shone directly on the stage, causing too much glare for the shoot to continue.

After growling in frustration, Mr. Frank shouted, "Ok! Let's break for lunch. No one's to leave the set. We'll provide you with sandwiches and coffee."

The photographer again rushed toward the stage to hook up with Sherry. Before he reached her, two hulking bruisers grabbed him roughly by the arms and snarled, "Didn't Miss Silver just tell you to get lost?"

"Hey, let go of me," protested March. "I'm the one who saved her."

"That's our job."

"Then, where were you durin' the fire?"

"Never mind. Get outta here while you still got legs to walk on."

Dylan saw it was useless to argue. With a dejected frown, he stumbled away to gossip with the journalist reenactors. These men were full of wisecracks and good humor, and the time passed quickly while they waited for the direct sunlight to rise above the stage. Finally, around one o'clock, the participants took their places and got ready for Take Two.

The second take had just begun when a freak gust of wind knocked over the drummer's cymbals. The third attempt was equally futile. Sherry had just launched into her wailing vocals when her microphone went dead. They had to scratch the fourth take after a Union reenactor's musket blew up in his face. So it went all afternoon until the fuming director postponed the shoot indefinitely.

Only Dylan was still grinning as the crew filed away from the Devil's Den. Not only did he have enough photos of the shimmying Sherry to please any gossip mag on the planet, but he also had the exclusive story of why her video shoot failed. He wasn't much of a writer, but he didn't need to be to report this juicy scoop.

The photographer sprinted to his car and leaped behind the wheel. Screeching out of his parking space, he almost ran over the cursing Mr. Frank. "Watch it, jerk!" the angry fellow barked. "I oughta have you arrested!"

"Bite me!" shouted Dylan. "Watch where you're walkin'!"

Before the director could summon security, March shifted gears and sped down Crawford Avenue well ahead of the other traffic. He passed safely through the roadblock, turned right, and blasted onto the main road. The rest of the drive was a blur. All he could think about were thousand dollar bills. And paying off his ex — for good!

Back at the motel, March set up an impromptu darkroom in his bathroom. He threw a blanket over the window, plugged in a red lamp to see by, and mixed up chemicals in the sink. When he immersed his negatives in the solution, he got quite a surprise. Instead of Sherry Silver in her provocative bikini, Dylan had shots of a gaunt figure dressed in Confederate gray floating in front of the pop princess. He also had photos of the ghostly soldier cutting the bass amp chord with a bayonet and tipping over the drummer's cymbals with his rifle butt.

"Whoooeee!" cried Dylan. "I can see the headlines now: 'Silver Video Ruined by Battlefield Ghost.' Man, when these pics hit the tabloids, I'm gonna be even more famous than Alexander Gardner."

With trembling hands, March finished developing his film. After hanging up the photos to dry, he locked his door and went outside for a breath of air. He was quivering with excitement and drenched with sweat. To cool off, he went to the lounge to have a rum and Coke. He downed the booze in one gulp and then cooed to the cute waitress, "I'll have another drink, darlin', 'cause my luck's about to change. Maybe you an' me could hook up later? What do ya say?"

"Sorry. The motel has a strict policy against dating customers."

"Ah, come on," wheedled March, fondling the girl's arm. "I'm gonna be rollin' in dough. Don't ya wanna help me spend some of it?"

"You'd be better off asking my grandma," replied the waitress with a stony frown. "She's about your age. Being a widow for ten years, she even might be hard up enough to go out with you."

"Ahh, forget that other drink," grunted Dylan, rising angrily from his chair. "When my pics are published, I'll have a whole limo full of chicks like you."

"Blind ones, no doubt."

"Ah, bite me!"

"Yeah, right after I get the manager."

Stifling a curse, the photographer stormed from the lounge and flew back to his room. He slammed the door and locked it behind him. Flipping on the overhead light, he flung his suitcase on the bed and began packing furiously. "I better get outta here before that mouthy chick gets me in trouble," he seethed. "After I blow this joint, I'm gonna order me one of them Latin babes whose only English words are 'Yes, Daddy.' "

Dylan stuffed his clothes in his suitcase without bothering to fold them. He just thought about retrieving his precious photos when a thunderous knock echoed through the room.

"Open up, March!" commanded a gravelly voice.

"Yeah, we know you're in there!" growled another man.

"I'm not feeling well," squeaked Dylan. "Come back in the morning. I'm sorry what I said to your waitress. Honest."

"You're gonna be a lot sorrier if you don't open up."

185

"Come back in the morning, I say."

The words were barely out of Dylan's mouth when his door came crashing open with the sound of splintered wood. Before the photographer could dodge into the bathroom, two thugs dressed in black military garb rushed to corral him. The burlier of the goons grabbed Dylan by the arm and twisted it violently behind him.

"Y-y-you're not the manager," wheezed March. "Y-y-you must be the 'associates' Bitchzilla's lawyer threatened me with."

"That's right, and we're here to collect your ex's thou. Where is it?"

"Well, what if I don't have it?"

"Then, we're gonna hurt you real bad," promised the burly professional, twisting Dylan's arm until he squealed like a girl.

"Okay. Okay. Enough!" whined the photographer. "Show a little patience. I'll have your money in the morning. I just gotta fax a few photos I took today."

"What kind of photos?" asked the second goon suspiciously, scratching the cobra tattooed on his forearm.

"Of a ghost."

"Yeah, right!"

"A battlefield ghost. Honest!"

"You ain't ever done anything honest," snarled the bulkier thug.

"But I swear it's true."

"Then, I wanna see 'em."

"Only if you quit. . . hurtin' me."

The thug released Dylan and then shadowed him into the bathroom. The photographer rubbed his arm to get the circulation flowing again before reaching to pull down one of the dry photos. "There!" he said smugly, handing the pic to the lawyer's man. "That one alone will pay the blood money I owe."

"Hey, what are you tryin' to pull?" asked the brawny fellow, grabbing Dylan roughly by the wrist.

"Pull?"

"Yeah, this picture's blank."

"Blank? That's impossible!"

"See for yourself."

Dylan stared aghast at the washed out, overexposed pic. Yanking free his wrist, he reached to pull down the rest of his photographs. A horrified expression spread across his face when he found them all ruined.

"Them photos are worthless," snarled the goon. "We'll just have to take your camera instead."

"But how will I make a living?" cried Dylan. "Isn't there some other way?"

"It's your camera or your hide," sneered the associate, slamming March against the wall until his teeth rattled.

"Okay! Okay! It's in the trunk of my rental car. H-h-here's the key."

"You better not be lyin'. . ."

The goon stalked out the door and returned a few minutes later holding a smashed camera by its cut strap. "No wonder them pictures was no good if ya took 'em with this hunk of crap," he laughed.

"But my Nikon was in perfect working order when I popped the film out of it. Did you drop it?"

"An' piss off my employer? Uh! Uh! It looks like there's only one way left to pay your debt."

"A-a-and what's that?" whimpered Dylan, noting the wicked gleam in the brute's eye.

"Ever gargled with this?" replied the professional, grabbing March's bottle of developing chemicals from the bathroom sink.

"But that's poison."

"Yeah, in your hands it is," cackled the tattooed goon. "It killed your photos deader than hell."

"But I couldn't have screwed up," bleated Dylan. "After the thousands of photos I've developed, I got the procedure down to a science. I know the time each step takes and exactly the right mix of chemicals and distilled water—"

"That's your problem right there, sneered the bigger thug, unscrewing the top of the acid bottle. "You shoulda used it full strength. Like this."

Dylan shrieked as his torturer dribbled a few drops of the solution on his bare arm. "Stop!" he cried. "Pleaseeeee!"

Watching March's skin blister, the tattooed goon said, "I wonder what'd happen if we filled the sink full of this stuff and dunked in his whole hand?"

"My thoughts exactly," muttered his partner. "I'll bet his ex will never be short of dough again. Let's try it an' see."

"No! No!" pleaded Dylan. "I-I-I got friends I can borrow the money from. I'll have it tonight."

"That's more like it," snickered the hulking associate. "To make doubly sure we get the entire thou, we're gonna dunk your hand anyway."

"B-b-but that's not fair."

"Like cheatin' on your alimony is."

"You get away from me, or—"

"Or you'll what? Scream?"

"Hey, that's what the Reb soldier in the parkin' lot's waitin' to hear," grunted the tattooed goon as he wrestled Dylan toward the sink. "If he hadn't told us

188

where you was holed up, we'd have missed out on all this fun."

"He sure was helpful, all right," grinned the burly associate. "March, when are you gonna learn to keep it in your pants? It don't pay to mess with these reenactors' wives. Hey, I'll yank down the curtain so that Reb can watch us burn ya. There he is. Right behind your car."

"No! Wait! That's the ghost I photographed."

"Tell it to the tabloids," snarled the tattooed thug, forcing March's hand into the acid. "After this, you'll never be late with another payment, will ya, pal?"

THE PRICE OF A PINT

The hobo rubbed his arms and muttered incoherently as he glanced toward a trash bin overflowing with greasy newspapers and broken cardboard boxes. Even if he bedded down there again tonight, he'd probably freeze to death, for this was the coldest November ever. According to the flashing sign outside the Tenth Avenue Bank, it was already one degree below zero at six p.m. What he really needed was a little "antifreeze" to brace himself against the cold.

But how was he, Raymond Bartholomew, to afford such a luxury as the price of a pint? With heating bills on the rise, people just weren't as generous as they'd been last summer. Lately, a whole week's panhandling barely netted enough for an occasional cup of coffee. Even worse, business was so slow in most restaurants that they weren't hiring dishwashers. Without that money, he'd even lost his bed at the flophouse.

Raymond began to pace furiously back and forth across the alley he now called home. His face was a blur of tangled whiskers, and his hair protruded wildly from beneath a clownish bowler hat. His once fashionable suit was stained and tattered. With the layers of grime caked on his skin, he looked vaguely Negroid lurking in the shadows.

There was always the possibility of a discrete mugging or two to keep a fellow going, but Raymond was much too squeamish for that. Besides, the only people weak enough for him to handle were either school children or senior citizens. Over the years he'd treated too many of those folks to find harming them very palatable.

Raymond dug his freezing hands deep into his pockets and wandered onto Tenth Avenue. As he stumbled past a row of dark store fronts, he stared through their barred windows at the same warm overcoats and luxurious sweaters that had once hung in his own closet. Finally, he came to a halt in front of Falcon Brothers' Liquors. It was the only place on the block still open, and the warm lights glowed inside like an expensive whiskey in the bottom of a crystal tumbler.

The hobo opened the front door and slipped into the shop. Casually, he examined several shelves of gift liquors in colored bottles while casing the joint. The proprietor, a burly bare-armed man, had risen when he came in and was now studying him in the ceiling mirror just overhead.

Raymond sidled around a display of dinner wines and proceeded up the brandy aisle. Glancing into the mirror, he saw that his every movement was being logged by the big hulk behind the cash register. Oh well, if he couldn't swipe a pint, at least he was going to take his time and get warm.

Raymond spent a good ten minutes peering at the various brands and flavors of brandy—a liquor of which he had recently been a connoisseur. When his hands finally began to thaw, he reached out to "inspect" a preferred bottle more closely. His fingers had no sooner closed around it when a heavy paw thumped down on his shoulder.

"May I help you?" growled a voice close to his ear.

"Just looking," Raymond replied with a twitchy smile. "I see you have my favorite brandy in stock."

"Gee, am I ever relieved to hear that. Would you like to *buy* a bottle to take with you?"

"Uh. . .Yes, I would, but. . .unfortunately I forgot my wallet at home."

"Yeah, I know. And your broker's out of town, too."

Rough hands seized Raymond by the collar and the seat of his pants, and he was given the bum's rush out into the street. He skipped nimbly across the sidewalk until crashing headlong into a trash barrel set out along the curb. When he came to moments later, he found himself sprawled in the gutter covered with coffee grounds and rotted fruit.

Not bothering to brush himself off, Raymond got to his feet and weaved drunkenly back to the liquor store. Damn! His assailant hadn't even waited to see how much damage he had done. He was back behind the cash register ogling a girly magazine.

Raymond staggered away from the door and started down the block. His vision was blurry, and his lips felt swollen. What was he to do?

Wiping the corner of his mouth, he came away with his palm smeared with blood. "God, and all along I thought I was slobbering on myself again," he muttered. "What a waste of good blood. What a. . . Hey! That's it! That's it!"

Raymond quickened his pace as he entered a dingy neighborhood comprised mainly of tenement houses. This was the dark side of the city unlit by streetlights or the hope of salvation. Only the most desperate sort of white men dared venture here, and Bartholomew cringed as shadows flitted past him reeking of day-old whiskey and vomit cologne. Several times he heard shrieks emit from the bowels of an adjacent alley. Then, he understood why people turned their heads and walked away from daylight stabbings.

Three blocks into the darkness, the hobo came to a low, professional-looking building illuminated by a single bulb over the doorway. He pressed the buzzer, and a nurse appeared on the other side of a barred window. She peered cautiously past him into the street. Seeing he was alone, she opened the door latch electronically and motioned for him to enter.

Raymond found himself in the shadowy anteroom of Roma Corporation, one of a dozen metro companies in the business of buying and selling blood. The need for such companies always existed in a city of two million people, for there were never enough donors to meet the needs of a diseased population prone to violent accident and heinous crime. What is more, Roma and its counterparts weren't too particular about the type of scabrous lowlife from which they obtained their blood supply. Filling the quota was always the bottom line. If they had to set up headquarters in the middle of a ghetto, so be it.

The same nurse who had admitted Raymond to the premises emerged from behind a hospital screen and took a seat at a dented, metal desk. Producing an official-looking form, she nodded toward an empty chair. Her movements were brisk, and her eyes were sympathetic as flint. When Raymond was seated, she snapped, "Name?"

"Raymond Bartholomew."

"Address?"

"Uh. . .Tenth Avenue."

"Have you given any blood in the past month?"

"No."

"Are you presently taking any medication?"

"No."

"Have you been out of the country recently?"

"No."

"Do you have hepatitis, syphilis, AIDS, or any other communicable disease?"

"No."

"Have you drunk any alcoholic beverages in the past week?"

"No."

"Okay, make your mark here and go down the hall to your right."

"Wait a minute," said Raymond coldly. "I'm very capable of *signing* my name."

"Then, *sign* here."

"Before I do, I'd like to know what this is for."

"It's a simple release," droned the nurse. "Will you hurry up? I haven't got all night."

Bartholomew approached the desk, snatched up a pen, and scribbled his signature. During the entire interview, the nurse hadn't looked at him once.

"Before I go through with this, how much will I be paid?"

"Between thirty and forty dollars. It depends on your blood type. Now, will you make up your mind?"

Swallowing hard, Raymond nodded his assent and then passed along a darkened corridor and through a pair of swinging doors. He emerged into a large, well-lit room furnished with padded tables. Several of these were occupied by elderly residents of the ghetto.

Oh well, thought Raymond as he glanced about. *At least I should get top dollar for my Type O blood.*

An ugly black nurse approached Raymond and led him to the nearest table. She instructed him to take off his coat, roll up his sleeve, and lie down. She scurried to a medicine cabinet, returning momentarily with a needle, a hose, a tourniquet, a plastic bottle, and a container of rubbing alcohol. She wrapped the tourniquet around Raymond's arm and gave it a couple of twists. Then, without warning, she sterilized a spot on his forearm and rammed the needle home. Before he could even yelp, she withdrew and reburied it a second time. She tried twice more to hit a vein before calling out in frustration to an elderly nurse. By that time, her patient had become strangely pale beneath the coats of grime on his face.

A testy white woman stormed over to Raymond's table and jerked the needle from the other nurse's hand. "Why can't they send me anyone but student nurses?" she raged as she successfully tapped a vein with one vicious poke of the needle. At that moment Raymond must have lost consciousness, for later he couldn't remember watching them hook up the plastic sack into which his blood was dripping.

Bartholomew closed his eyes, but the nightmare didn't go away. No matter how many liquor bottles he conjured in his mind, he couldn't blot out the stale smell of urine wafting from the black fellow next to him.

God, how unfair life can be, reflected Raymond. *To look at me now, who would ever believe that only last fall, I was the one examining patients on padded tables? Somehow, washing dishes isn't very satisfying after twelve years of college, medical school, and specialized training in pediatrics. Nor is being a social outcast, for that matter. . .*

But how else was I to examine the girl for VD? Of course, I should have never agreed to treat her without first notifying her parents. That was stupid! Yet, when you deliver a child into the world and see her through the measles, mumps, and chicken pox, you do feel a certain

195

responsibility toward her. I guess I should have been less concerned about her embarrassment and more concerned about my reputation.

Still I can't see how anyone could get sexual satisfaction from a simple medical examination, as she later claimed. A little rich girl might say anything, though, to keep from losing her allowance. Why should she care that I got expelled from the A.M.A. for sexually deviate behavior with a minor and would never practice medicine again?

The other patient began to moan softly, and Raymond peeked in his direction. The old Negro was gripping his arm just above where the needle protruded from it. With sweat shimmering on his black skin, he reminded Raymond of a stereotypical slave from a second-rate Civil War movie. The only difference was that his master, the ghetto, hadn't needed whips or chains to inflict the required amount of suffering.

Raymond studied the needle sticking from his own arm. *I still must be in shock,* he reasoned. *Otherwise, wouldn't I feel some kind of pain? Just think how many blood samples I took without once considering how frightening it was for the patient. Oh well, at least tonight I'll be able to return to the liquor store and buy* **two** *pints of brandy. Won't that clerk be surprised to see me again? Maybe the SOB will even apologize when I flash a little green. Then, I'll get a hotel room and sleep until noon under* **real** *sheets. And won't a nice hot bath feel good? And a shave? Why, I'll even get my suit cleaned and pressed! Then, I'll look like a proper--*

"Hey, mista! You! Hey!"

Raymond woke with a start and discovered his ugly black nurse hovering over him. She was tapping his shoulder impatiently while glancing at her watch.

"Yo time's up," she growled, "an' you won't git paid."

196

"Excuse me?"

"Look at yo sack, mista. You ain't but half filled it. Didn't they tell ya we only pays for a full unit?"

"You mean if I don't give a whole pint, I don't get any money?"

"That's right! Looks like we's just gonna have to pack it back in ya."

"Pack what back in me?"

"Yo blood. Now, you lay still. This is gonna hurt some."

The nurse raised the plastic sack even with her head, and the blood began flowing back down the long tube. The hobo winced and grabbed his arm. This time shock did little to dull the pain. When the sack was empty, the nurse yanked the needle free and slapped a band-aid over the still oozing hole. Pointing to the side exit, she said, "Okay, you can go."

"Go?"

"Are you deaf besides bein' a po bleeda? I said git outta here!"

Suddenly, Raymond felt very angry. He had gone through a lot for the price of a pint, and he wasn't going to be cheated. Brushing aside the nurse, he rushed over to a cart loaded with fresh blood. Before the staff could recover, he tore open a container and chugged it in a single gulp.

By the time Raymond had finished his second bottle, the entire room was in an uproar. Nurses were screaming. Buzzers were ringing. Patients were bellowing. One old black man became so frightened, he dove under a table, dislodging the needle from his arm. In seconds, the floor was flooded with blood squirting from the plastic sack.

The head nurse rushed through the swinging doors in response to the alarm bell. Spotting Raymond, she wasted no time. With a grunt, she hurled herself at him, planting her fingernails in the middle of his back. Bartholomew shrugged her off as if she were an opinion with which he disagreed. There was a strange gleam in his eye. His mouth was rimmed with crimson. With a single bound, he hurdled the table between him and the side exit. In another, he was out the door. Tenth Avenue was soon to become a very unsafe place for weak, warm-blooded beings.

THE CRIMSON TINGE

Johnny pulled up in front of a purple mansion that sat sandwiched between two vacant brick homes. The painter did not shut off the motor right away but sat surveying the three-story dwelling with a professional eye and a foot poised over the gas pedal. He had heard all the wild rumors about the place, and he had a hard time disbelieving their validity as he studied the garish purple walls and barred windows. It didn't help matters that the rising sun shone directly on the freshly painted house front, accenting its odd crimson tinge.

Johnny ran his hand across the two-day stubble sprouting on his face before turning off the ignition. A rumpled ball cap covered his unruly shock of snowy hair, and his soiled painter's clothes were dotted with faded splotches of tan and blue. "Shouldn'ta took this gol-durn job," he grumbled as he climbed down from the patched seat of his pickup and hobbled around to yank open the sagging tailgate.

The truth of the matter was that Johnny hadn't worked all summer and was in no position to turn it down. He had botched several jobs the painters' union had set up for him earlier in the year, and they had pretty much written him off. . .until now. They had also conveniently failed to tell him that everyone else at the union hall had passed on this particular assignment after the first two painters had mysteriously disappeared from town. All that Johnny knew was that he had received one thousand dollars in advance just to finish part of a back wall.

Johnny hoisted a forty-foot ladder from the rack atop his pickup and weaved beneath its weight toward the spiked fence that surrounded the house. Fortunately, the gate had been left open, and he moved cautiously through it and then past six heavily curtained, barred windows around to the back of the house. The lawn felt spongy as cemetery grass beneath his feet.

With a grunt, the old man dropped the ladder and raised his eyes to study the back wall of the house. The other painters had scraped the entire surface with an expert skill far beyond that now capable of his stringy muscles and creaking joints. They had even burned off some of the more stubborn chipped spots before priming and painting the back peak. Their work had stopped just above a curious oval stained glass window located two-thirds the way up the clapboard wall. Amber in hue, it was approximately three feet wide and five feet high. It was also the only window on that side of the house and the only one with no bars or curtains.

It took all the old man's strength to hoist the ladder into position well away from the window. "Get the gol-durn thing eventually," he muttered while returning to his truck to retrieve a four-inch brush, two gallons of paint, and a drop cloth to spread on the ground beneath the ladder. Sure it was against standard procedure to do the lower part of the wall before finishing the window, but Johnny figured he might as well get the grunt work out of the way first.

Johnny knelt at the foot of the ladder and opened one of the unlabeled paint cans with his putty knife. Then, he withdrew a wooden stick from his coveralls and mixed the paint with an unhurried lifting motion. It took many minutes of patient stirring to blend in the queer, crimson swirl that had separated from the rest of the mixture and accounted for its abnormal hue. If this paint had not been sent with his thousand dollar check, Johnny knew he couldn't have matched it with any enamel he'd run across in forty years.

"Musta had the gol-durn stuff imported," reasoned the old man as he examined the contents of the unlabeled can once more before starting up the ladder behind him. When he reached the top, he fished in his coveralls and produced an S-shaped hook that he employed to hang his paint pail from a convenient ladder rung. Then, he pulled a brush from another pocket and began applying the paint in long, smooth, practiced strokes. One coat covered the clapboards within his reach, and he climbed down to move the ladder closer to the window. He repeated the procedure twice more until he was two feet from the amber orb. At that point, he swung the ladder two feet to the other side of the window and continued across the side of the house. Afterward, he moved the ladder below the window to the next tier down. By so avoiding the fine trim work, he was able to finish the entire back wall by lunchtime.

Johnny returned to his pickup and snapped open a dented lunch pail. Since his wife died in '82, he had lived primarily on junk food, and today was no exception. As he wolfed down a bag of potato chips and a cold can of greasy spaghetti, he sat contemplating the crimson-tinged purple house with an unexplainable dread. There was just something about that color that gave even an unimaginative man like Johnny the heebie-jeebies.

Shifting his gaze from the gaudy porch to the barred windows above it, the painter could have sworn that he saw the curtains part and then quickly close. With a shiver, he tossed the half-eaten can of spaghetti back into his lunch pail and rooted under the seat for a trim brush. He produced a paint-caked screwdriver, three pop bottles, and a moldy submarine sandwich before he finally located one.

"Time to get this gol-durn place done and get the hell outta here," growled Johnny when he returned to his workstation and stared up at the two-foot unpainted strip of clapboard surrounding the single window. "Gonna be a bitch, but I gotta do her!"

Johnny adjusted the ladder and raised it even with the top of the window. After again stirring the paint, he climbed upward until he could reach the unpainted circle to the right of the amber orb. Then, he dipped his brush, wiped away the excess purple globs, and proceeded to, as they say in the painter's trade, "cut in" the stained glass pane. Although his hand shook with palsy, he used a skill gained through forty years of experience to deftly complete the task.

The old painter moved the ladder to the left of the window but did not scale it right away. Instead, he walked around the yard on his toes to stretch his aching arches and calf muscles. What he really needed was a quick nap, but somehow the thought of sleeping in the lengthening shadows of that odd-colored house wasn't exactly appealing. Also, the sky had become more overcast as the afternoon progressed, and the sun disappeared behind the clouds with alarming frequency. It was this observation that finally prodded Johnny back to work. One thing was for sure. He definitely didn't want to get rained off and have to return tomorrow!

While Johnny began to climb the ladder, the sun emerged from the clouds and reflected from the clapboards back into his eyes. Half-blinded, he squinted toward the amber window to get his bearings. It was at that exact moment that the sun again dipped out of sight.

Johnny found himself staring straight into the center of the stained glass pane, which was constructed like a human eye. Looking through the pupil, he could distinctly see an attic loft of considerable dimension. Hanging upside down from the rafters of the vaulted ceiling were two human forms dressed in painters' coveralls. Tubes ran from each of the dangling arms into open paint cans on the floor.

Johnny grew faint and slumped forward against the ladder. As he did so, he dropped his bucket, spilling its contents down the side of the house. Clutching madly at the rungs above him, he managed to right himself. Before he fully regained his senses, he felt an added weight on the ladder below him. Somehow, he dared not look down. . .

THE BUD MONSTER

Had I known what was to follow, I never would have agreed to feed the Fraisers' cat while they were on vacation. Yet, what could I do? Gossip had it that my next door neighbors' marriage was in trouble. When they told me how their trip to Myrtle Beach was to be a second honeymoon, I felt compelled to oblige. Although I've lived alone for over twenty years since my dear Eloise passed away, I guess I'm still a sucker for romance.

I'd seen their sneaky cat stalking baby rabbits in the backyard, and it had sickened me to watch her tear a cuddly bunny to shreds. I must grudgingly admit she was a pretty creature, though, with greenish-yellow eyes and a decorative white patch on her neck and chest.

"We call her Bud," said my neighbor's wife with a flirtatious wink, "because she absolutely loves people."

"Yeah, her name is short for Buddy," added Mr. Frasier. "But you'll have to be careful, or she'll take advantage of you. Especially be sure to ration her food. She'll chow down the whole bag if you let her."

"I can tell she's an eater," I replied. "I swear she's the largest house cat I've ever seen."

"And could you do one more thing for us? Pretty please."

"What's that, Mrs. Frasier?"

"Could you shoo the cat away from the road if you see her out there? You know how dangerous the traffic can get on Highway 5."

"Now, don't you worry about. . .Bud. I'll take good care of her. Just go and enjoy your stay at the ocean."

That evening I heaped the cat's plastic bowl with fish-shaped dry food and set it on my back steps like I had promised. The bowl no sooner left my hand when the huge tabby fur ball came bounding from the neighbors' shrubs to pounce on the feast like a miniature lion. I chuckled as I watched her feed greedily and then laughed aloud when she abandoned her empty dish to rub contentedly against my legs.

"What an appetite you have!" I scolded. "You eat more than two cats!"

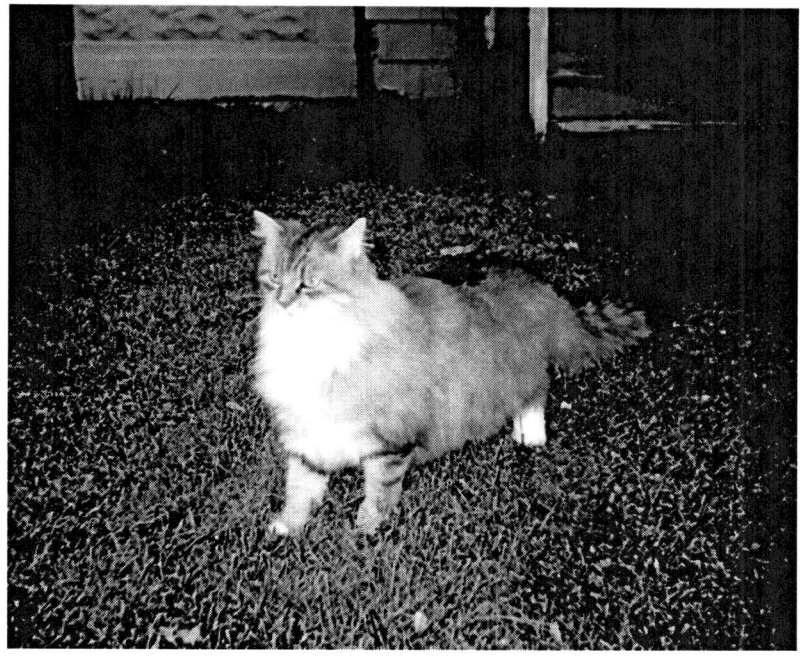

Then, I made the mistake of picking up Bud to stroke her fur and gibber nonsense to her. She clung to me in total adoration, snagging her claws in my best sweater. When I set her down, I had the hardest time pushing her away so I could get inside my screen door.

With her owners gone for a week, Bud decided to adopt me. Every morning I found her waiting on my back stoop when I went out to buy a newspaper. And in the evening, there she was again. As soon as my Ford pulled in the driveway from my daily trip to the Senior Center, Bud would streak mewing to greet me. She rubbed against my legs and got under my feet every time I crawled out of the car. Sometimes she even leaped in my lap if I didn't slide out from under the steering wheel quickly enough. Then, she tried to follow me into the house. I had the hardest time holding her off with one leg while I slipped through the door. I had no rest even then because the crazy cat whined and whined until I came out with her supper dish loaded with food.

After a few days, I was so sick of Bud's unwanted attention that I seriously considered checking into a motel until the dang feline's owners returned from Myrtle Beach. Unfortunately, even that didn't solve the problem because the Fraisers split up soon after their honeymoon vacation. I'm not the nosy type, so I don't know the particulars. I did, however, notice that one evening there was plenty of screaming over at their place followed by a visit from the local police. Before it was over, my neighbor's wife boiled out of the house and slammed two suitcases into the trunk of her red Corvette. "So what if I do have lots of male friends?" I heard her bellow. Then, she sped off, never to return.

Mr. Frasier wasn't home much after that. His lawn went unmowed and his cat unfed often for weeks at a time. That made Bud an even more permanent fixture on my back stoop. Now, what was I to do? I was renting my house, and the landlord, who owned three beautiful Persian cats himself, disapproved of his tenants having pets.

"Animals make too much of a mess," he had said the day before when he stopped to pick up the rent and saw how Bud rubbed against my legs while he and I chatted in the driveway. "I can't allow my renters to have pets, or I'd have to replace the carpet every time someone moved out. I'd never make any money on this place."

After I had lied about only watching Bud temporarily, I worried all night that my landlord would kick me out if he learned how much time the cat really spent at the house. He lived two doors up the road, so it wouldn't be difficult for him to spy on me. I was only paying two hundred dollars a month, which stretched my pension as it was. But even though I would be in a world of trouble if I had to move elsewhere, I still found it difficult to be mean to an abandoned animal. I just wished her demonstrations of love for me weren't so obnoxious and obsessive.

I guess I'm just an old softy because the very next afternoon I let Bud come in out of the weather during a terrible thunderstorm. That was another big mistake. She immediately made herself at home, peeking behind the couch and into cupboards and closets. Even worse, she followed me around like a Seeing Eye dog. She loved to scoot through my legs and remained so close underfoot that she kept tripping me. I couldn't even go to the bathroom without her tagging along.

She became such a pest that I went to the refrigerator and cut her a piece of cheese. After dangling it in front of her nose, I led her to the back door and chucked her treat outside. Off she shot to pounce on the delicious morsel in total disregard of the drenching downpour.

"Tricked by your own greed, you crazy cat," I shouted after her. "See if you come in this house again."

But come in again she did! My arthritic, old bones could never slam the door fast enough whenever she'd ambush me on my return from the fitness walks Dr. Weinstein prescribed for my heart condition. All I wanted to do then was shed my sweaty jogging suit and crawl into a nice tub of hot water. Instead, I had to play hide-and-seek with Bud, who scooted in the house before me to disappear beneath the bed or behind the entertainment center where she wrapped herself in stereo wires and TV cords.

Yep, Bud had a habit of appearing at the most inopportune time, all right. Whenever I came home from shopping and had to lug heavy sacks of canned goods up the back steps, there she'd be right beneath my feet tripping me up. Then, she'd streak into the kitchen to swish her tail contentedly while I cursed her tabby hide under my breath. Of course, she had to poke her nose in every grocery sack to see what was inside. If I didn't watch her carefully, every time she ended up with the fish sandwich I bought at the deli. Once she even jumped onto the kitchen counter and knocked a jar of pickles onto the floor. The jar smashed into a million little pieces that I kept stepping on and embedding in my feet for months afterward.

One day after Bud almost upended me down the cellar staircase, I punted her like a hairy football off the porch. She hit the ground hard and then dove into my neighbor's untrimmed hedge to sulk and hiss. She didn't come around for a couple of days after that until hunger got the better of her. Then, she was back mewing, mewing, mewing over *The Price Is Right* until I finally broke down and let her in. She naturally showed her appreciation by sharpening her claws on my new recliner and getting muddy footprints on a freshly-washed bedspread. When I bent to swat her on the head, she hissed so menacingly that I resorted to the treat-out-the-backdoor-trick to finally get her to leave.

Bud's sudden viciousness shook me up so much that my pulse rate jumped way out of control. As I gobbled down a glycerin pill, I seriously began thinking of ways to rid myself of that greedy, green-eyed beast forever! What if I lured her into the car with some catnip and then dropped her off in a neighboring town? How about giving her to the SPCA? Or maybe I could borrow my brother's German shepherd to chase her away. Of course, that might get me evicted if Bruno tore into my landlord's cats, too! They sometimes came over to play with Bud although they were too skittish to ever approach the house.

As I continued to consider my options, Bud again began mewing furiously on the back stoop. Gritting my teeth, I went into the kitchen and busied myself with a sinkful of dishes that I should have washed days ago. I had just begun scouring the pans when I heard the cat banging against the front door. Her fit intensified until she became impossible to ignore. Finally, she came and sat with her back to me just outside the kitchen window where she couldn't help but be noticed. I could tell by her posture that she was angry. My dear Eloise used to get her back up the same way whenever she thought I wasn't paying her enough attention.

If I'd have been a crueler man, I would have spiked that cat's food with rat poison long ago. Instead,

I went to the door and let Bud in. She immediately began circling my legs and rubbing against me until I picked her up and stroked her fur. "You're creepy and kooky and altogether ooky," I sighed. "What am I going to do with you?"

I set the cat on the floor and began cuffing her playfully. Then, I teased her with a piece of cheese. Every time she sprang to grab it, I pulled it just out of her reach before offering it again. Finally, Bud leaped up and planted her fangs deep into my wrist. Blood oozed from my punctured skin, and I yelped in surprise. This time the cat did not follow me when I made a beeline into the bathroom to pour peroxide on the wound. I had heard of people getting cat scratch fever, and I wasn't going to be one of them. After wrapping several layers of gauze over my wrist, I made up my mind once and for all to rid myself of that vicious beast!

I grabbed a broom from the closet and rushed into the kitchen. I expected to find the cat cowering in a corner or whining defensively near the door. Instead, she leaped on my shoulder from atop the refrigerator, slashing wildly with her claws. I felt a searing pain in my left eye and toppled backward onto the table, smashing it into kindling. The monster continued to slash my eyes until both pupils were rendered useless. Then, she leaped aside, hissing and snarling like a thing possessed, while I punched blindly at thin air.

Finally, adrenalin kicked in, and I leaped to my feet like a Senior Olympian. I careened across the kitchen, groped through the living room, and ripped open the front door. With Bud's horrific caterwauling still ringing in my ears, I leaped off what I remembered to be the porch. Afterward, I bolted into total darkness toward the roar of traffic on Highway 5. I'm sure the driver who hit me had no time to stop. I only wanted away from the Bud monster, no matter what the cost!

Now, I lie in the hospital with my blind eyes bandaged and my broken legs in traction. In an effort to console me, the nurse says it's a beautiful, sunny day. She also says she has a special surprise that involves a visit from my landlord and a furry friend.

"What do you mean by f-f-furry friend?" I stuttered aghast.

"Why, your cute, cuddly cat. Your landlord has been taking care of it for you, and he plans to bring it over during visiting hours. He didn't have the heart to send it to the SPCA after all you've been through. We normally don't allow animals in the hospital, Mr. White, but we thought we'd make an exception this time. Now, doesn't that make you feel better?"

THE LONG WAY HOME

"Look out the window," said Mrs. Anderson with worry etched on her kind face. "The snow's really coming down. I think you should forget my painting and get home while you can."

Desmond Jones set down his paint pail next to the living room archway where he was working. Wiping his hands on his splattered bib overalls, he peered out at the fierce blizzard bombarding the neighborhood. Not only was the snow thick, but the wind whipped it sideways to create whiteout conditions.

"You're right, ma'am," replied Jones with a nervous smile. "But I'll pick up my drop cloths first."

"No, just go ahead, Dessie. I'll straighten up. You have dangerous hills to travel."

"Thanks, Mrs. Anderson. I'll clean my brush and be on my way. I'll bet school lets out early this afternoon. I'd like to get out of town before the slick roads are clogged with all that bus traffic."

Desmond strode to the kitchen sink and ran warm water on his two-inch cut brush. Staring out at the raging squall, it seemed to take forever to rinse the white paint from the bristles. White always stayed in the brush longer, anyway, and Jones had to bite his tongue to keep from cussing. He surely didn't want to offend the nice Swedish lady who had hired him in the middle of a very tough winter, so to stem his impatience he hummed a Jimmy Buffett tune until the job was complete.

Returning to the living room, he found Mrs. Anderson holding his coat and tool box. "Have a safe trip," she said. "Call me when you get home, so I won't worry."

"Yes, ma'am. Thanks for everything."

When Desmond opened the front door, a gust of wind nearly bowled him over. The Anderson home was built on a side hill, and he skated down a slick set of steps to snow-covered Belleview Avenue below. There was already a foot of heavy slop on the ground and no sign of it letting up.

The painter yanked on his gloves, brushed off the side door of his Ford Taurus, and inserted his key in the lock. The lock was frozen and wouldn't budge, so he hustled around to the passenger door. Again, he stuck the key in the lock and vigorously turned it until it finally clicked. The door itself, however, was encased with ice. He reefed on the handle with all his might before the door finally swung outward with a grating creak.

Fetching his scraper from the dashboard, Jones scurried about like a monkey as he cleaned off the windshield. The snow was coming down so hard that he barely completely the task when he was forced to start over twice more. Finally, in disgust, he leaped behind the steering wheel, fired up the engine, and turned the windshield wipers on full to clear his vision for his hazardous drive.

Desmond eased his Taurus in gear and crept along Belleview Avenue. The street was unplowed, and he could only manage five miles an hour without skidding toward the row of parked vehicles lining the curb. Belleview wound parallel with the hill and then made a sharp right turn to plummet to the street below. When Jones tried to negotiate this curve, he slid dangerously toward a ditch that ran between the road and the last house on the street. Pumping his brakes, he stopped just before his car careened into the snowy trench.

Sweat soaked his face as Desmond backed his vehicle onto the flat lane above the curve. Carefully cutting his wheels, he started forward at two miles an hour and again skated toward the ditch. Wildly, he spiked the brakes, only stopping inches from disaster. After backing up a second time, he then rolled down the hill at one mile an hour. The street had become even greasier from his spinning wheels, and his Taurus slid almost sideways before he got it under control.

With frustration glittering in his eyes, Desmond jerked his car in reverse and spun up the hill for another try. His stomach churned, and his hands trembled on the wheel. Several cars were behind him now, too, waiting to exit Belleview. In his side mirror he could see the lips of the impatient drivers dissecting his incompetence. No one was going to move until he did, so he put aside his anxiety and once more eked his Taurus into low gear.

Jones kept way to the left on this descent and finally steered clear of trouble. Keeping his foot on the brake, he inched down the steep hill toward Jackson Avenue where a steady stream of school buses rolled past. He didn't dare go any faster, or he'd skid into the flow of traffic and cause a horrific accident.

It took Desmond ten minutes to go a hundred yards. When he finally reached the foot of the hill, his body shook, and a vague headache throbbed in his temples. Luck was finally with him, though, for a bus stopped up the block, and children began spewing out its folding door. This allowed Jones to pull directly onto Jackson Avenue and head for home.

Although Jackson was a main artery through Bradford, it, too, was extremely slick from the steady, falling snow. "Dang!" muttered Desmond as he crept along. "If it's this slippery in town, what's Red Rock Hill going to be like? Any other day, I'd be back in Duke Center by now."

The painter continued to go no faster than ten miles an hour down the busy rush hour street. He pumped his brakes well before each stop sign because he knew from years of winter driving that stopping and starting vehicles turned intersections into skating rinks. By using extreme caution, he was able to reach Bolivar Drive without incident. There, the traffic thinned, so Desmond speeded up to fifteen and headed into the country.

The weather became more severe with each mile Jones drove. When he finally reached the little village of Derrick City, he could barely see twenty yards ahead of him. Drifts were now piling up in the road, making the going even tougher. Each time he hit one, it reminded him of riding his fishing boat through rough waves. Wiping the steam off his windshield, he peered anxiously ahead. Everywhere, snow coated the trees, obscuring the most prominent landmarks. To the painter, even the oil jacks looked cold.

I shouldn't have come out today, Desmond thought, as he plowed through the deepening ruts. *But how could I disappoint a customer who feeds me lunch every day and treats me like a son? I have a reputation for reliability, too. If I had a dollar for every time the weather man was wrong, I could retire to the Florida Keys.*

Desmond kept a slow, steady pace until he came to the junction of Derrick and Rock City Roads. There, a squad car with flashing red lights blocked the highway. A shivering officer dressed in a summer uniform jacket and a pointed hat signaled for him to stop and turn around.

"So is Red Rock Hill closed?" asked Jones after cranking down his side window.

"No, I'm auditioning for the Eskimo Club," growled the freezing policeman. "Why else would I be out here?"

"Are any of the roads to Duke Center open?"

"What do you think, Buster? Look at this crap come down!"

Instead of responding with a snappy comeback, Desmond punched the gas. Blasting slop from his churning wheels, he spun his vehicle in a circle and fishtailed back the way he had come. Glancing in the side mirror, he could see the splattered policeman shaking his fist at him. Jones chuckled with satisfaction and then muttered, "That'll teach that SOB! Maybe he'll be nicer to the next guy who asks him a simple question."

As Desmond pushed toward Bradford, a worried frown crossed his thin face. "What should I do now?" he wondered aloud. "With all the hills closed, I'll never get home. Unless. . ."

Jones increased his speed to twenty miles an hour and bucked and spun his sturdy Ford through the last few snow-clogged miles to Route 219. There, he crept up the on ramp and merged with a steady stream of passenger cars and big rigs headed due north. After he settled into line, he said with a grin, "Why didn't I think of this before? All I gotta do is take the long way home through Olean, Portville, and Eldred. It's flat the whole way. If I take it easy, I'll be in DC well before dark."

Desmond's smile suddenly evaporated when a semi closed hard on his back bumper and began blowing a series of strident horn blasts. The highway was so slick that he had again slowed to fifteen, but the trucker behind him drove like it were summer. Jones was hemmed in on the left by an oil tanker, and the sweat stood out on his brow as the two trucks squeezed him. Finally, the tanker inched past, and the other semi whipped out into the passing lane with its trailer weaving dangerously behind it. Dessie slowed even further and crowded the slushy berm to keep from being sideswiped. The trailer missed his Taurus by inches as it swayed past, while the trucker issued another salvo from his air horn.

When Jones reached the Cow Palace exit, he took it. Tears streamed from his eyes, and his nerves were frayed to the limit. As he again headed back to

Bradford, he croaked, "Only one chance left. G-g-guess I'll try Looker Mountain."

The road crews were hard at work in the city when Desmond arrived there. The sand trucks sent orbs of yellow light spiraling from their rooftops as they spread their gift along the streets. This settled the painter down. He turned with renewed hope onto South Kendall Avenue and started toward home through a steady curtain of sleet.

The sleet now presented a new challenge that Dessie's windshield wipers couldn't handle. Soon, he was forced to pull off the road and knock the ice from the rubber wiper blades, so he could see to drive. He only managed a mile or so before his visibility was severely challenged, and he stopped to repeat the process. He finally drove out of the nasty precipitation just as he reached the turnoff for Looker Mountain Trail.

This road was a total mess as the wind drifted snow and created whiteout conditions. All Desmond could do was keep his car between the guardrails and forge on. To quell his apprehension, he muttered, "Man, am I glad they invented front-wheel drive. If I had the old Maverick, I'd be rotta ruck. Don't know how many times I spun sideways up over the hill in that heap. That was when I worked second shift at Case Cutlery, and poor Betty Kervin rode back and forth with me. She got so nervous when we'd start to skid, she broke into fervent prayer."

Jones chuckled at the memory and then stared through his fogged windshield at the long straightaway leading to the foot of the mountain ahead. Snow plastered the trees on either side of the road, making a grim tunnel through which to roll. Gunning his engine, he accelerated to forty miles an hour to begin his ascent up the long, gradual slope. He had his gas petal jammed to the floor and only let up on it if he started to slide.

"Got a good run for the hill!" he cackled. "Just hope my speed holds."

Desmond continued to make decent progress until he reached the right curve half-way up the mountain. Here, he churned past numerous wrecked vehicles slammed up against the guardrails. Many of the cars were so smashed that it looked as though they'd been rammed. Yet, there were no multi-car pileups that would cause such damage. Even more curious, he passed no drivers looking for help.

With his hands in a death grip on the wheel, Desmond reached the last steep incline leading to the top of the mountain. Yelping, "Bonsai!" he again tromped on the gas and surged forward as his tires churned and smoked and sprayed snow. His vehicle climbed with urgency now because a silver SUV was blasting along behind him for all it was worth.

When Jones' Taurus finally spun to the summit, the four-by-four on his tail shot past him and careened down the Rixford side of the mountain. "What got into that crazy fool?" Dessie grunted as his windshield again iced over, this time on the inside. "Hey, where'd the road go? Hey!"

Before Desmond could grab his scraper from the dashboard, he found himself sliding out of control on the icy, downhill slope. Pumping his brakes only worsened the problem, so he downshifted into low. Out of instinct he hit the brakes when he continued to skid. This caused him to spin in a complete circle and slam backward into a ditch. Shrieking in terror, he ripped open his door and scrambled from behind the wheel. After wiping blood from a cut on his cheek, he stared wide-eyed at his wrecked car. It looked as though the ditch had eaten his Taurus by the way it protruded from the yawning hole in the snow.

Jones turned up his coat collar and stomped dejectedly back to the ridge top. He panted with fatigue and felt sick inside. Soon, he heard an engine laboring up Looker Mountain Trail, so he turned to stare down the treacherous slope. He didn't wait long before a yellow PennDOT sand truck came chugging up the hill toward him. Desmond's chapped lips cracked into a relieved smile, and he waved and shouted to attract the driver's attention. As the vehicle rumbled nearer, Dessie saw that its blade wasn't down. No sand was spewing from the back, either.

"Is that fellow drunk, or what?" raged the painter to the gusting wind. "Is—"

Jones' other question stuck in his throat when he spotted a huge mane of white, shaggy hair in the oncoming cab. Black, clawed fingers clutched the wheel, and glowing, yellow eyes glowered at him hungrily through the shattered glass where a human head had smashed the windshield. He then knew why there were so many battered vehicles littering the hill and why the SUV passed him on the summit at maniacal speed.

"It's the Abominable Snowman drivin' that truck!" screamed Desmond. "The Abominable freakin' Snowman!"

ABOUT THE AUTHOR

William P. Robertson was born in 1950 in Bradford, PA. He graduated from Mansfield University in 1972 with a B.S. in English. He has since worked in factories, taught high school English, and run a successful house painting business. In his spare time Bill enjoys following the Pittsburgh Pirates and fishing for vicious muskellunge. Robertson began freelancing short stories, poetry, and articles in 1978, and his work has now appeared in over 490 magazines worldwide. He has also collaborated with David Rimer on a series of historical fiction novels about the famous Civil War rifle regiment—the Bucktails. For more information about Bill's writing, visit his website at http://bucktailsandbroomsticks.com.

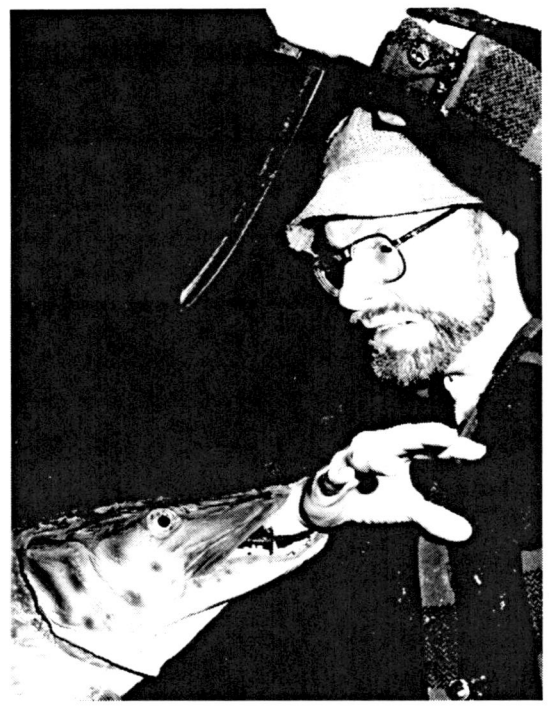

ALSO FROM INFINITY PUBLISHING

Lurking in Pennsylvania collects three decades of William P. Robertson's best horror stories and poems, many of which appeared in magazines worldwide. In this anthology Bill writes understated Gothic terror in the tradition of Lovecraft and Poe. He draws his material from local legends, his grandma's Swedish folktales, and traumatic personal experiences. He also delves into dark humor and lends a fresh perspective to the werewolf and troll. Bill's best work chills rather than sickens. To order an autographed copy of *Lurking in Pennsylvania*, send $15.27 (postpaid) to William P. Robertson, P.O. Box 293, Duke Center, PA 16729. Make checks payable to Bill Robertson.

ALSO FROM INFINITY PUBLISHING

Dark Haunted Day is William P. Robertson's second collection of macabre tales. As the title indicates, ghost stories are the focus here. A gallant battlefield ghost, a malicious college phantom, and two spectral husbands are just a few of the hobgoblins haunting this anthology. Again, the author selects such Pennsylvania settings as Gettysburg, Mansfield, and the ever-spooky McKean County for his action. To add variety, a hunting horror story, a psychological thriller, and a Kinzua Viaduct death tale prey on the reader's imagination. Characters range from kids to the elderly, and all get their share of scares. To order an autographed copy of *Dark Haunted Day*, send $15.27 (postpaid) to William P. Robertson, P.O. Box 293, Duke Center, PA 16729. Make checks payable to Bill Robertson.

ALSO FROM INFINITY PUBLISHING

Terror Time is William P. Robertson's third book of suspenseful stories and eerie photos and poems. Variety is the key to this collection as the author explores such themes as obsession, revenge, and debilitating fear. A demon-possessed alcoholic, blood-crazed bullies, and a drug-pushing witch are just a few of the villains that spur the action forward. Hailing from Western Pennsylvania, Robertson squeezes the chills from many local situations and legends, as well. The dangers of winter driving, for example, fuel two of his tales, while the ghost haunting Smethport, PA's Old Jail sets up shop in another. The author also brings back his Bucktail Civil War characters, Bucky Culp and Jimmy Jewett, to star in two "Eastern Westerns." These edgy historical fiction yarns feature plenty of gunplay, horse chase scenes, and a stagecoach stickup. *Terror Time* ends with "Evil Love," the author's first foray into dark fantasy. Robertson's books may be ordered from Infinity Publishing at www.buybooksontheweb.com.

BRITTLE SHADOWS

In the Gothic gloom of December,
fresh graves settle in the constant sleet.
I revel in the stench of squashed lady bugs
and listen to termites tunnel through my boots.
The only joy is found in the faces of the dead.
The only sunshine casts brittle shadows.

CPSIA information can be obtained at www.ICGtesting.com
Printed in the USA
BVOW04s2054101013

333446BV00006B/60/P